Was it love?

Ryan had his son, Sawyer, to think about. But Danielle and Sawyer already shared an easy affection that would grow if fed time and patience. In short, loving Danielle might not be such a bad thing for the boy...*or for him.*

So why did the thought scare Ryan half to death?

Maybe it was because what was between them defied logic, common sense and caution. Near strangers, they had kissed in the dark and tempted fate. And he'd enjoyed it way too much.

Was this a Christmas miracle? A little Yuletide magic? A gift from above that Ryan would be a total idiot to deny?

He didn't know...but he was going to find out.

Linda Varner brings you the joy of the holiday season with three very special couples who discover a HOME FOR THE HOLIDAYS...and forever.

WON'T YOU BE MY HUSBAND? (11/96)
MISTLETOE BRIDE (12/96)
NEW YEAR'S WIFE (1/97)

Dear Reader,

What better way for Silhouette Romance to celebrate the holiday season than to celebrate the meaning of family....

You'll love the way a confirmed bachelor becomes a FABULOUS FATHER just in time for the holidays in Susan Meier's *Merry Christmas, Daddy*. And in *Mistletoe Bride*, Linda Varner's HOME FOR THE HOLIDAYS miniseries merrily continues. The ugly duckling who becomes a beautiful swan will touch your heart in *Hometown Wedding* by Elizabeth Lane. Doreen Roberts's *A Mom for Christmas* tells the tale of a little girl's holiday wish, and in Patti Standard's *Family of the Year*, one man, one woman and a bunch of adorable kids form an unexpected family. And finally, *Christmas in July* by Leanna Wilson is what a sexy cowboy offers the struggling single mom he wants for his own.

Silhouette Romance novels make the perfect stocking stuffers—or special treats just for yourself. So enjoy all six irresistible books, and most of all, have a very happy holiday season and a very happy New Year!

Melissa Senate
Senior Editor
Silhouette Romance

Please address questions and book requests to:
Silhouette Reader Service
U.S.: 3010 Walden Ave., P.O. Box 1325, Buffalo, NY 14269
Canadian: P.O. Box 609, Fort Erie, Ont. L2A 5X3

MISTLETOE BRIDE

Linda Varner

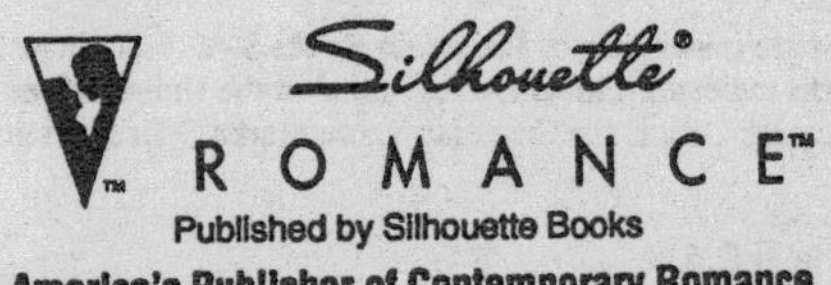

Published by Silhouette Books
America's Publisher of Contemporary Romance

Thanks to Ginger Moix for sharing her expertise on horses, barns and rodeos.

ISBN 0-373-19193-6

MISTLETOE BRIDE

This edition published by arrangement with Harlequin Books S.A.

Printed in U.S.A.

Books by Linda Varner

Silhouette Romance

Heart of the Matter #625
Heart Rustler #644
The Luck of the Irish #665
Honeymoon Hideaway #698
Better To Have Loved #734
A House Becomes a Home #780
Mistletoe and Miracles #835
As Sweet as Candy #851
Diamonds Are Forever #868
A Good Catch #906
Something Borrowed #943
Firelight and Forever #966
**Dad on the Job* #1036
**Believing in Miracles* #1051
**Wife Most Unlikely* #1068
†Won't You Be My Husband? #1088
†Mistletoe Bride #1193

*Mr. Right, Inc.
†Home for the Holidays

LINDA VARNER

confesses she is a hopeless romantic. Nothing is more thrilling, she believes, than the battle of wits between a man and a woman who are meant for each other but just don't know it yet! Linda enjoys writing romance fiction and considers herself very lucky to have been both a RITA finalist and a third-place winner in the National Readers' Choice Awards in 1993.

A full-time federal employee, Linda lives in Arkansas with her husband and their two children. She loves to hear from readers. Write to her at 813 Oak St., Suite 10A-277, Conway, AR 72032.

Recipe for
A Very Merry Christmas

1 cowboy
1 newly found son
1 unexpected mugging
1 independent single gal
1 rescue
1 ranch (big enough for 3...or more)

Toss together cowboy and son, add in Christmas Eve mugging. Stir in single gal and a reluctant rescue. Set mixture on an isolated ranch, right in time for Christmas morning. Simmer until too hot to handle.

Yield: A *HOME FOR THE HOLIDAYS*...and forever!

Prologue

"Okay. You don't have to go if you promise me that you won't play with matches, stick anything in your nose or ears, drink poison or open the door to strangers." Ryan Given, now hesitating on the threshold of the motel room he'd just rented, hated leaving his son, Sawyer, alone for even a second. It was something he hadn't done since they'd found one another.

"Aw, Dad," responded the boy, who lay sprawled on his stomach on one of the beds, his nose a couple of feet from the television set. "That kind of stuff is for kids. I'm eight years old."

"So you are," Ryan hastily murmured, properly chastised. Though his fingers itched to tousle Sawyer's dark hair affectionately, he wasn't that comfortable with the boy yet, so dared not. Instead, he stepped into the freezing cold night and shut the door firmly behind him. Sawyer would surely be okay for the fifteen minutes required to walk to a nearby café, pick up their take-out dinner and walk back to the motel. In fact, he'd probably be okay for longer than that. He was damned mature for his age.

Grinning with fatherly pride—a novel experience—Ryan sidetracked to the narrow metal strongbox hidden behind the seat of his pickup truck, where he'd stashed their traveling cash. He tucked a couple of ten-dollar bills into his wallet, then headed to the café where a long overdue hearty meal awaited. He and Sawyer had been on the road ten hours, with only quick snacks to nourish them. Both wanted the works tonight: salad, fried chicken, mashed potatoes, homemade cloverleaf rolls with lots of real butter, apple pie and ice cream....

Ryan swallowed hard and stepped faster, his face stinging from the brisk winter wind. Wishing for his sheepskin-lined jacket, which hung in the motel room, he noted how dark it was for 7:30 p.m.—black as pitch, thanks to heavy snow clouds—then glanced toward his destination, the Clearwater Café. Though a tree-tangled shortcut obscured his view of the building, Ryan could tell that vehicles filled the back parking lot. He couldn't help but wonder why all these people weren't at home, spending Christmas Eve with their families.

Ducking to avoid a low-hanging limb, Ryan entered the shadowy no-man's-land that would save him steps, according to the motel desk clerk. Almost instantly, he stumbled over a rock, invisible under the patchy snow underfoot. Then a frozen tree branch slapped his cowboy hat off his head. Staggering like a wino on a cheap drunk, Ryan reseated his hat, then forged a path through the gnarled branches by pushing them, crackling and popping, away from his face.

So much for saving steps, he thought as his hat left his head again. Cursing his bad luck, Ryan bent to retrieve it.

He heard the snap of a frozen twig. He sensed that he was not alone.

"Who's there?" Ryan blurted out, words that barely left his lips before he saw a blur of motion and felt pain shoot through his head.

Chapter One

Humming "Blue Christmas," the last song she'd heard inside the Clearwater Café that Thursday night, Danielle Sellica slipped behind the steering wheel of her car and set her one-more-for-the-road cup of coffee in the plastic holder designed for it.

She wrinkled her nose at the smell of old grease and cigarettes that permeated her denim jacket. Although a few minutes of fresh Colorado air would easily kill the scents, Dani didn't get out of the car. It was already 8:30 p.m., and a one-hour drive home still lay ahead. Not that Dani minded the drive. She really didn't. There was just so much to do before she could go to bed tonight—not the least of which was put up and decorate her Christmas tree.

A mood as blue as the Christmas of the song settled over her. Refusing to give in to it, Dani turned on the radio and quickly found a station playing something upbeat. She relished the cheerful tune, as well as the beauty of the snowflakes dancing in her headlights, for only a moment before turning the volume way up so she could sing "Holly Jolly Christmas" at the top of her voice.

It was the buzz of the car phone that brought an end to her off-key songfest some forty-five minutes later. Since only one person ever called her on the car telephone—bought for emergency purposes only—Dani smiled and turned off the radio, then snatched up the receiver.

"How did you know I was in the car?" she demanded, instead of saying hello.

The familiar laughter of Jonni Lisa Maynard, a dear friend and neighbor, spilled forth. "Lucky guess."

"Do I hear Jimmy Stewart in the background?"

"Of course. Have I ever made it through December without crying over *It's a Wonderful Life* a couple of dozen times? For that matter, have you?"

It was Dani's turn to laugh. They were both sentimental softies for sure. "No to both. Are you ready for Christmas tomorrow?"

"I'm proud to report that my presents are wrapped, my fruitcake is baked and my tree is up. How about you?"

"I'm not into fruitcakes, but my shopping, such as it is, is done."

"What about your Christmas tree?" asked Jonni.

"The most beautiful Douglas fir in the world is in my trunk even as we speak. I'll put it up the minute I get home."

"And I thought I was running late! Any big plans for the holiday?"

"I'll probably sew."

"You mean you still haven't finished Barbara's wedding dress?" Jonni asked, referring to a mutual friend who planned a New Year's Day wedding.

"Another lucky guess," Dani told her, ruefully adding, "Would you believe she's changed her mind about the sleeves *three times?*"

"I'd believe that. What I cannot believe is that you ever agreed to make it in the first place."

"Temporary insanity?"

"Well, that beats the permanent kind, which is what I'll be by the time Ricky goes back to school." Ricky was Jonni's rambunctious seven-year-old son, out of school for the holidays and already driving his mother nuts. She also had a four-year-old daughter named Pattie and was trying for a third child.

"Which reminds me—"

Thump. Thump.

A sudden sound, loud enough to make Dani abandon what she'd started to say about having presents for the children, seemed to be coming from the rear of the car. A flat? she automatically wondered with a mental sigh of dismay.

"Dani? You still there?"

"I'm here, and I've got a flat," Dani replied even as she braked her car and eased off the asphalt.

"Oh, God," Jonni exclaimed, clearly concerned. "Will you be okay?"

"Are you kidding? I can change a tire in five minutes with one hand in my pocket." She didn't add that she'd never had to do it on a lonely mountain road with the heavens spitting snow....

"Well, be careful. Two guys broke out of prison this morning—"

"Thanks so much for letting me know," Dani retorted dryly, refusing to think about a prison break at Cañon City, less than fifty miles away.

"Oh, honey, I'm sorry—"

"I was teasing you. I'm not a bit scared. Now, I really have to go."

"Please call me when you get home. I'll worry until I hear from you."

"I'll call," Dani promised, wishing her friend a Merry Christmas before hanging up.

With another sigh, this one of resignation, Dani killed the engine. After checking to see that the car was easily visible to approaching traffic, should there be any, she switched on the hazard blinkers. Flashlight in hand, Dani then got out of the car.

With purposeful strides, she walked around her vehicle, inspecting each tire in turn. There was no flat. Had she imagined that awful noise...?

Thump! Thump! Thump Thump Thump! As if on cue, it came again, only louder.

Dani whirled toward the sound, which seemed to be emanating from the trunk. For the first time, she noticed that Kyle Smith, the surly teenager who'd loaded her Douglas fir in the trunk, had not tied down the lid as she'd requested, but had closed it instead.

Wondering if something besides a Christmas tree now lay inside, Dani retrieved her keys from the ignition. Had that bad-mannered young man played some sort of practical joke on her? Dani wouldn't have been surprised. He'd made it more than plain that carrying a Christmas tree from the service station, where she'd bought it, to her car, parked behind the café next door, was beneath him. Obviously she should have supervised the task instead of heading inside the eatery for her late dinner.

Though admittedly more outraged than afraid—some poor stray dog or cat was probably trapped inside the trunk—Dani did clutch the long-handled flashlight like a club. In truth, she was fully prepared to trounce whatever she found, should it prove dangerous.

Her ring full of keys jangled against the car when she inserted the right one in the lock—

"Thank God!"

Dani squealed and leaped back at the sound of the muffled masculine voice coming from inside her trunk.

"Hey!" Thump! Thump! *"I'm dying in here! Let me out!"*

She could not move. She could not think. For the first time, fear shimmied up her spine. How could this be? Had Kyle somehow fallen in . . . ?

Or was one of the escaped convicts hiding in her trunk?

"Hel-looo? Anybody there?"

Heart hammering, Dani eased the key out of the lock. Not for anything was she going to open this trunk now.

"I know you're out there. Open up, dammit." Thump! Thump! *"Open up now!"*

With a gasp, Dani spun on her heel and lunged for the driver's side of the car. In a heartbeat, she was behind the steering wheel. In another, she was speeding back to Clearwater. Destination: the police station. More than once, Dani glanced fearfully in the rearview mirror, half expecting to find a man in a bright orange jumpsuit with a number stenciled on it sitting in the back seat.

But he was in the trunk, not the back seat.

"Omigosh!"

What seemed an eternity later, but was really only forty minutes, Dani turned on two wheels into the parking lot adjacent to the Clearwater police station.

She greeted the officer on duty, Cliff Meeks, by name—they went back a long way—then spilled her story in a rush of words. Without comment, Cliff rose from the cracked-vinyl swivel chair and headed straight down the hall to the exit that opened onto the parking lot.

"You don't even seem surprised," Dani commented, hurrying after him.

"Nothing could surprise me tonight," drawled the relocated Texan, an old friend of Dani's father. She didn't have time to question the cryptic comment before they reached her car. Silently, Dani handed him the key. Then she took cover behind his considerable girth.

Instead of opening the trunk, Cliff slapped his hand down hard on the lid. "Hey in there! Chief Cliff Meeks, Clearwater Police, speaking. I want your name, and I want it now."

"Ryan Given. Let me out."

"Okay, Mr. Given, I will. But you should know that I'm armed, so don't try anything funny."

"I swear I won't," came the muffled reply. "Just let me outta here."

His expression unreadable, Cliff pulled his gun, unlocked the trunk and tossed back the lid. Inside lay a man, as expected—a wide-shouldered, broad-chested, long-legged man. Dani took quick note of his clothing—western from head to toe—before dragging her gaze away.

A cowboy. A sweet-talking, good-looking, don't-worry-yore-pretty-li'l-head-about-it cowboy. She'd be safer with an escaped convict.

This cowboy's groan of agony drew Dani's gaze back to him. Without sympathy, she watched as the blue-eyed wrangler untangled his feet from a length of rope and unfolded himself from the trunk. It took an assist from Cliff, who for some reason had reholstered his weapon, to get the stranger fully on his feet. Then the man sat right back down on the rim of the open trunk, touching his fingertips to the back of his head. Dani saw blood on them.

"It's about damn time," the ungrateful stowaway commented, glancing at his blood-smeared hand. He looked accusingly from Cliff to her and then back to Cliff. "Are we really still in Clearwater after driving around for so long?"

"That's right," Cliff said, coolly adding, "ID, please."

The man, clearly in a temper, shook his head. "Stolen by whoever locked me in here. I'm from Tulsa, Oklahoma, staying at the Garrett Motel. My eight-year-old son is with me...back at the motel, I mean. I told him I'd just be gone a minute—"

"You left an eight-year-old child alone in a motel room?" Dani blurted out in horror. If that wasn't typical cowboy logic!

Ryan Given never wasted so much as a glance on her. "He's probably wondering where I—"

"Sawyer is inside the station, Mr. Given. We picked him up two hours ago at the Garrett when the clerk called to report your disappearance."

Ryan's jaw dropped. *"Two hours ago!"* He glanced at the back of his wrist as though he usually wore a watch, which he didn't now. "What the hell time is it?"

"Ten o'clock."

"Damn!" Ryan leaped to his feet and immediately stumbled forward as if his legs were asleep. Or was he just dazed from his head wound? Dani wondered as both she and Cliff made a grab for him.

"Whoa, fella. Better take it easy," Cliff said.

"But Sawyer—"

"Is just finishing two quarter-pound burgers, double fries, a large cola, and a fried pie. That boy can really put it away."

Dani felt some of the tension leave the cowboy's body. "You fed him?"

"We fed him." Cliff grinned. "That's quite a youngster you've got there, Mr. Given. Thanks to his description, I knew that you were who you said you were the minute I saw you," the policeman continued, words that explained the reason he'd reholstered his gun.

Ryan relaxed so completely that Dani's shoulders dipped under the weight of his muscled arm, now stretched across them.

"Dani, can you hang around long enough to give me your version of what happened tonight?" Cliff asked.

"I guess so," she replied somewhat grudgingly. In truth, she wanted nothing more than to hightail it back to the sanctuary of her ranch. Dani, who worked hard to make her life an endless cycle of identical days, didn't want or appreciate the excitement fate offered her this Christmas Eve.

At that reply, Ryan Given disengaged himself from both her and Cliff. When Dani automatically put distance between them, the cowboy gave her a once-over so thorough her entire body glowed with embarrassment. His expression said that what he saw did not impress him. Dani, who *shouldn't* have cared less, nonetheless bristled.

"I guess I should thank you for bringing me back to Clearwater," Ryan said. He put his fingers to the back of his head again and winced. His comment did nothing to soothe her ruffled feathers. His discomfort evoked no compassion.

"Don't bother. I only did it because I thought you were one of the convicts who escaped this morning." She turned to Cliff. "Have they been caught yet?"

"No, but it's just a matter of time. We put out an APB right after the motel clerk saw them steal Mr. Given's truck—"

"They stole my truck?"

Cliff nodded, his own expression full of the empathy Dani lacked. "We thought they'd taken you, too, as a hostage...speaking of which, your son is anxious for your safety. Why don't we go on inside? I'll tell you everything I know there, and we may even be able to rustle up another hamburger or two."

Looking a little dazed, Ryan nodded. The two men then followed Dani into the station.

A good twenty minutes passed before Cliff, Ryan and Dani finally sat down in the break room to reconstruct the night's events. She paid for her earlier lack of pity for Ryan by now blinking back tears that resulted from the emotional, if oddly restrained, reunion she witnessed between the cowboy and the young son who obviously adored him.

Admittedly interested in Ryan's brief tale of attack, blow to the head and subsequent awakening—bound and gagged—in the trunk of her sedan, she nonetheless gave him only half of her attention. Sawyer Given, now watching an old black-and-white television in a corner of the room, owned the other half.

For an eight-year-old, he displayed remarkable maturity, she thought, recalling how solicitous he'd been of his father. Dani was not surprised by what appeared to be a role reversal. She was quite familiar with the phenomenon, having once cared for an irresponsible single parent such as Ryan.

That the man was single, she could only assume, of course. At any rate, there was no wife-mother on the scene, and neither Ryan nor Sawyer had mentioned one. Clearly, the boy was used to seeing to dear old dad. Dani resented the injustice, one she'd experienced herself as a fifteen-year-old when her rancher father died too young and her pampered mother, Eileen, became dependent on her.

Unbidden, scenes from the past, long suppressed, filled her head—scenes of cooking her own breakfast before school so Eileen could sleep late, scenes of nights at home alone while yet another sweet-talking man wined and dined her mother in town. Dani surfaced from the swirling eddy of memories with difficulty and only because she heard someone speak her name.

"Want to tell us your story now?" It was Cliff, and he sat with pencil poised over one of countless forms he'd undoubtedly have to fill out tonight.

"Not much to tell," Dani replied. "I parked my car at Clearwater Café around seven o'clock—"

"In the back lot?" Cliff asked.

"Yes, the front one was full. I saw the Christmas trees at Smith's Station next door, so I walked over there to get one before going into the café. I told Kyle—you know, Ed Smith's youngest?—to tie down the trunk instead of locking it so the branches wouldn't be crushed, then I went on inside the café to eat. It was awfully crowded, so I didn't get out of there again until eight-thirty or so."

"And you were where when you heard Mr. Given in the trunk?"

"Almost home," Dani said with a sigh, wishing she were there now. Every muscle in her body ached with fatigue—not surprising since her Thursday had begun at 5:00 a.m. "I was talking to Jonni Maynard on that phone you insisted I buy—" she gave Cliff a smile "—when I first heard him banging around back there. I guess he'd just woke up."

"Actually, I'd just freed my hands and was trying to get your attention," Ryan grumbled. "I couldn't make myself heard over your serenade."

Dani glared at him to cover her embarrassment at being caught singing. "I turned off the radio the moment the phone rang. Why didn't you try again then?"

"I wanted to hear what you had to say." He shrugged. "I thought you were the one who locked me up."

Dani huffed her opinion of that. "You've got to be kidding."

"I hadn't seen you, remember?"

Apparently, he could tell she wasn't physically capable of hoisting him into the trunk. "I was referring to the radio.

Didn't you think it odd that someone who'd just mugged you would then sing Christmas carols all the way home?"

"Hell, lady, I—"

"Can't you say a word without cursing?" She shot a meaningful glance at Sawyer, whom she considered to be at a very impressionable age.

To Dani's surprise—she expected a "Mind your own business!"—Ryan followed her gaze. He flushed beet-red. "Sorry, ma'am. I guess I left my manners in the trunk of your car." Looking somewhat subdued, he turned to Cliff. "Sawyer and I are in the process of moving to Wyoming, Chief Meeks. We're going to buy ourselves a ranch there. Everything we own but one suitcase was on that truck, including our traveling cash."

"We'll do our best to get it back," the chief said. "We're beginning to get some information on the prison break now. I've had a phone call from a tourist who gave two guys in street clothes a ride from Cañon City to Clearwater. I'm pretty sure they were our men."

"I'm just glad I didn't clean out my savings account when we left Tulsa," Ryan murmured with a shake of his head. "My boy and I'd be in a mess for sure—"

"You realize that your bank won't be open again until Monday, don't you?" The question fell off Dani's tongue before she could stop it.

Ryan's smile vanished.

"That's three whole days away," Dani continued. "What are you and your son going to do until then?"

"Oh, we'll be okay," Ryan told her, an idiotic reply if Dani had ever heard one.

How like a cowboy to play his cards close to his vest, Dani thought. Well, this time she didn't need to peek over his shoulder to see what hand fate had dealt him. She *knew*. So did Cliff, if his frown was anything to go by. Dani waited for the kindhearted chief of police to invite Ryan and Sawyer home with him. Instead, he rose and motioned for her to follow him into the hall.

"How many horses are you boarding now?" he asked her when they were out of earshot of Ryan Given.

"Ten, counting mine," she replied, wondering where on earth this was headed.

"Hmm. Running any cattle?"

"You know very well that I am."

"Then I'll bet you could use a little help around that place of yours...what with that big wedding of Barb's just around the corner."

Dani's stomach began to knot. Surely Cliff wasn't going to suggest—

"Why don't you take Mr. Given and that boy of his home with you? They could help out for a while in exchange for room and board."

Dani's jaw dropped. This man, of all people, knew how she felt about cowboys, especially cowboys looking for homes on the range. "Are you kidding? I don't even know this man. He could be a wife beater, a drug addict or a drunkard. He might have stolen that child in there from his mother—"

"He's none of the above," Cliff gruffly interjected.

"And how do you know that?"

"Motel had his truck license number. I ran a check on it and then on him."

Dani sighed. Trust Cliff to be thorough.

"It's destiny that's brought him here. Destiny."

"What are you talking about?"

"I'm talking about you living alone at that oversize ranch of yours, doing the work of two men."

"I manage."

"Now, yes. But you can't keep it up, and you know it."

"I knew this would happen!" Dani raged. "I should never have asked you for advice when Mick sold my timber rights to Duke Littlejohn. Now you think you can tell me how to run all my business."

"Two heads are better than one."

Dani sighed again. "In a crisis like that, yes. Everything is all right now—or will be once I finish that stupid wedding dress. I simply have no use for some deadbeat cowpoke and his kid."

"He's not a deadbeat. He's just a little down on his luck. But forget him. Think of that boy of his . . . that eight-year-old boy. This is his first Christmas with his dad—"

"What?"

Cliff nodded. "I don't know the whole story . . . just that Sawyer and his dad met for the first time in September. Do you really want them to spend their first Christmas together on the street?"

"So let them spend it with you and Ruth."

"We've already got a houseful of her relatives or I would. You're their only hope, Dani, girl. You, and you alone."

"Don't do this to me," Dani groaned.

Cliff grinned, obviously sensing victory. "Just last week you were whining because you were going to be alone for the holidays. These guys'll be company for you—company for Christmas—not to mention help when you need it most. Come on, honey. What do you say?"

"I say a cowboy is absolutely the last thing I wanted for Christmas," Dani muttered as she turned abruptly on her heel and stalked back into the lounge. "Cliff seems to think you might be interested in working for room and board for a few days until you get your finances in order," she said to Ryan.

"You mean, you're looking for a hand?" he asked, perking right up.

"I haven't advertised, if that's what you're asking," she answered candidly. "I usually don't need help around the place. Right now, though, I have another project going on... a wedding... and I could use a little assistance."

Ryan sat in silence for a moment before he spoke. "When I left Oklahoma, I swore that the next ranch I worked on would be my own. Obviously that's going to have to wait. I appreciate your job offer, and I accept." Ryan stuck out his right hand, which she took after a moment's hesitation. Firmly he shook it. "Thanks, um, I don't believe I heard your last name."

"Sellica," she told him.

"*Miss* Sellica," Cliff added, a clarification that earned him a dirty look from Dani.

"But not for long...?" Ryan looked from one to the other of them, as though waiting for them to explain something.

For a second, Dani couldn't imagine what, then she figured it out. "The wedding I'm involved with is a friend's, not mine. I'm sewing her dress, which has to be ready by December thirty-first. I've had to neglect my ranch work while working on it."

"And now that we've settled that," Cliff said a little too heartily, "why don't the three of you hit the road? By the time you get to Dani's, it'll be half past Christmas."

"Damn!" Ryan blurted out, the next instant intercepting Dani's glare. "I mean *darn.* Sawyer's present was in the back of my truck with everything else."

"I have a remote-control race car you can give him," Dani said quickly, without thought, as she glanced at the young boy watching TV on the other side of the room. When Ryan looked at her in surprise, she realized what she'd said. Shrugging, she explained, "I bought it for the son of a friend."

"I'll pay you back." Clearly, Ryan was not comfortable accepting charity.

In spite of everything, Dani sympathized. Independent recognized independent. "Of course," she agreed. "Now, if we just had the Christmas tree your convicts stole from my trunk."

"They're not *my* convicts," Ryan muttered.

The sudden glint in his eye, coupled with the set of his chiseled jawline, startled her and hinted that there were other sides to Ryan Given than the side she now saw. Dani felt her stomach knot with uncertainty and something very like fear, the results of her dealings with another mystery cowboy not so long ago.

Swallowing hard, she vowed that this one would take his mysteries with him when he left on Monday. How could she be so sure? Because she would take no chances this time. Not for a moment would she let down her guard.

And because she would not, when Ryan and his son moved on, her ranch, her land, her money, and, most important, her just-repaired heart would still be intact.

Chapter Two

"How far is it to your ranch?" asked Sawyer, now nestled among Dani's groceries in the back seat of her car. Ryan glanced over his shoulder at his obviously excited son and smiled. Though working as a cowhand on some two-bit ranch wasn't at all what *he'd* had in mind on leaving Oklahoma, his boy clearly had no objections.

"Just fifty miles," Dani told him. "But it usually takes about an hour to get there because the last ten miles are steep and curvy. This snow isn't going to help us, either."

"Hey, Dad," Sawyer then said. "How's your head?"

"It's fine," Ryan replied. He did not touch the wound, which had been cleansed and was remarkably tender to the touch.

"I see bologna and bread back here," the boy said. "You want me to make you a sandwich?" Ryan had refused all offers of food at the police station.

"Those groceries belong to Miss Sellica," Ryan quickly replied, with a glance of apology to Dani. Once he and

Sawyer were alone, he'd make plain their destitute situation for the next few days and lay down the ground rules, the first of which was *take as little charity as possible until Monday*. That's when he'd call his bank in Tulsa and have some money wired to him. Just how difficult such a transaction would be now that he didn't have his savings book, his ATM card or even ID remained to be seen.

"Feeding you is part of the bargain," Dani tartly informed him and then glanced back at Sawyer. "I have a regular picnic in those sacks—paper plates, napkins, cookies, chips. Why don't you rummage through them and see what you can find for your dad to eat?"

"There's no need, Miss Sellica," Ryan began, even though his mouth watered at the thought of food.

"I insist," Dani coolly replied, adding, "And you may as well call me Dani since I intend to call you Ryan. We don't stand on formality around here."

"Right," Ryan murmured, once again put in his place. Damn, er, darn, but it rankled having a woman tell him what to do. Darn? *Darn?* Was he really censoring his very thoughts? Ryan flicked a glance of annoyance at Dani, the woman to blame.

Though not a beauty by any means, she had a nice enough face, what looked to be natural blond hair, cut short and shaggy, and big, brown eyes. Her shapeless denim jacket, which came nearly to her knees, hid what curves she had. A deliberate attempt to conceal her femininity? he wondered. And if so, why?

"Go ahead and make me a sandwich, Sawyer," he said, though his son was already rustling through the plastic bags of groceries. Ryan said it to remind Dani who was the parent here. The look she gave him said he'd made his point.

Just then, they passed the Clearwater Café, now closed and dark inside. At once Dani stomped on the brake. Muttering an apology, she began to back up the car so that she could turn into the deserted parking lot. Moments later, she killed the engine and fumbled to unfasten her seat belt.

"What are you doing?" Ryan asked.

"I'm going to see if I can find my Christmas tree. Whoever stuffed you in my trunk had to have left it somewhere around here." She felt all around on the floorboard of the vehicle. "What'd I do with my flashlight?"

"Forget the flashlight," he told her. "Forget the tree. It's too late to decorate it tonight, anyway. I'll get you another one tomorrow."

"With what?" she challenged, obviously referring to his lack of funds.

"With an ax," he replied. "You do have at least one pine tree on your property, don't you?"

"I have hundreds. I just prefer a Douglas fir for my Christmas tree. It's sort of a Sellica tradition." She sat in thoughtful silence, from all appearances in a real quandary about the switch in trees.

"For the sake of my aching head," he said, "could you please dispense with tradition just this once?"

She looked at him with some alarm, no doubt remembering Cliff's cautionary speech about possible concussions and certain headaches. "I guess a pine would be okay this year, but it'll have to be perfect."

"No problem," Ryan said. "We'll look until we find one, won't we, Sawyer?"

"Yeah!" the boy exclaimed, clearly delighted with the idea. And no wonder—up until now, they weren't going to have a tree at all.

Sawyer handed Ryan a paper plate that sagged with the weight of a thick sandwich, ridged potato chips, chocolate chip cookies and a giant dill pickle, plus a canned soft drink.

The can, which had probably been in the car for hours, actually felt cool to the touch.

"Good job!" Ryan told his son, adding a proud grin to the compliment. Though times were a little tough now and might be for a while longer, he wanted Sawyer to feel secure in his love, at least.

While he set his plate in his lap and popped the top of the canned drink, Dani refastened her seat belt. Soon they were speeding down the asphalt two-lane again. Though little but the black of midnight could be seen through the window, Ryan nonetheless cherished what he could make out of the landscape whizzing by. Moving out West was the right thing for him and Sawyer. He felt it in his gut.

And even getting off to this bad start did little to dampen his enthusiasm. Certainly having his truck and all his worldly goods stolen amounted to a major setback, but the vehicle was insured, after all. As for his "worldly goods," well, they didn't really amount to much more than old clothes, a few hundred dollars in cash and a box or two of memories. It was the last he'd miss most, Ryan suspected. Clothes and cash could be replaced. The photographs, rodeo trophies and belt buckles that represented the high points of his life could not.

But he still had his son, Sawyer. *Son.* Though an undeniable reality—Sawyer had Ryan's nose and his eyes—the concept of fatherhood continued to amaze him.

"Not far now," Dani commented, words that brought Ryan back to the present with a jolt of surprise. A quick glance at the clock on her dash revealed that it was almost 1:00 a.m. Another glance confirmed that Sawyer was asleep, his head resting on Ryan's jacket. Where had the miles gone? Had he, too, snoozed?

The car lurched sharply when Dani turned off the pavement onto a narrow, rutted and graveled road that disappeared into a dense stand of pines.

"We're on my land now," she said, pride in her voice. "A Sellica has lived on this mountain for ninety-four of the past one hundred years."

"How may acres do you have?" Ryan asked.

"Only half of the original homestead, thanks to my stepfather's getting the other half when my mother passed away three years ago."

Ryan noted that her reply told him nothing about the size of the ranch. A deliberate evasion of his question? he wondered. "And you work the place alone?"

"Easily."

They topped a small rise and her ranch suddenly lay before them, a loose gathering of buildings, all shapes and sizes, illuminated by a couple of strategically placed mercury vapor lamps. The main house was easiest to spot, since it was largest. There were several other buildings around it.

"That the bunkhouse?" Ryan asked as she braked the car to a halt near the side porch of the house. He pointed to a white frame building off to their left, which looked large for a ranch so small one woman could handle it alone.

Dani glanced off in that direction. "Yes."

"Good." He moved to get out of the truck.

"You and Sawyer can't sleep in there."

Ryan froze, his hand still on the door handle. "Why not?"

"Because it's full of junk, not to mention mice and who knows what other little varmints."

He waved away her concerns. "Just loan us a couple of pillows and blankets, and we'll be fine."

"No way." She killed the engine and shook her head. "The two of you sleep in the house tonight."

Ryan stared at her in disbelief and some irritation. He wanted to keep his debt to her to a minimum. "Lady, you don't even know me."

"So?" she retorted.

"So don't you think a little caution is in order, here? I could be six kinds of psycho."

"I could be, too."

"All the more reason for Sawyer and me to sleep in the bunkhouse."

"Are you saying you think I'd hurt you?"

"N-no, but—"

"We may as well clear this up right now," Dani suddenly stated, turning sideways in her seat and hooking an arm around the neck rest. "Do you do drugs?"

"Never have, never will."

"Ditto for me. Do you drink?"

"Only the occasional beer and not even that lately." He glanced over his shoulder at Sawyer.

"Same here. Have you ever robbed a bank?"

"Don't be ridiculous."

"Me, neither. How about murder?" she asked next. "Have you ever killed anyone?"

"Not no, but hell no," Ryan said.

"Hmm. Well, though sorely tempted at times—"

Like when he forgot himself and cursed? Ryan wondered.

"—I haven't, either. But is safety really the issue here? Or is it some misbegotten macho notion that you don't want to take more from me than you have to?"

Ryan winced. Women and their intuition! It drove him nuts.

"For the sake of that boy's Christmas," Dani continued, her voice little more than a loud whisper. "Please just do what you're told and stay with me tonight."

Ryan glanced back at Sawyer, still sleeping like a babe. At once all the fight went out of him, and he sagged with defeat. "For the sake of that boy's Christmas and only for that, I will."

"Thank you. Now, could we please go inside? I'd really like to get a couple hours' sleep before I have to get up again, and I still have to phone my friend, Jonni, who's probably out of her mind with worry by now."

"You're the boss," Ryan replied—truth that rankled, truth he suspected he'd rue long before Lady Luck smiled on him again.

Ryan woke around seven o'clock on Friday morning feeling rested. Try as he might to go back to sleep, he couldn't, and so crawled out of the narrow bed in which he'd slept. Dressed in a pair of jeans and a thermal undershirt, he tiptoed up the hall to make use of the single bathroom, then headed to the kitchen. Not hearing a sound, he assumed that Dani and Sawyer were still sleeping.

In a matter of minutes, Ryan located the coffeepot and coffee. He made short work of measuring out the grounds and the water, then set the pot on the stove and turned on the flame. While the coffee perked, he explored the front half of the house, which consisted of a dining room turned office, and a living room.

He liked the look of the place, which was too young to be antique, too old to be stylish, but just right, all the same. He saw no carpet on the wooden floors, just the occasional braided rug. The walls, most of them wallpapered in soft florals, were dotted throughout with what looked to be dozens of framed family portraits.

In the living room, Ryan spotted a pasteboard box labeled Decorations. Reminded that it was Christmas—a fact that had not crossed his mind yet—he walked back to his room, retrieved a heavy wool shirt from his suitcase and his boots from under the bed, and headed outside to what he assumed was the toolshed. With luck, he'd find an ax and chop down a tree before Dani even got out of bed, saving himself much traipsing around in the ankle-deep snow looking for the perfect one.

Ryan checked out the weather as he walked to the shed, noting with childish pleasure the cloudy sky and the crisp, clean smell of threatening snow. How he'd missed that smell the past twenty-three years. It was good to be home.

Home? Not by a long shot. Wyoming was their next home and no place else would do...even this picturesque Colorado ranch, nestled in the foothills of the Rockies.

Ryan reached for the door of the shed, only to hear the distinct *thwack, thwack* of an ax already in motion not too far away. Curious, he set out for the sound and in minutes came upon none other than Dani, chopping down a head-tall pine. She wielded the ax rather awkwardly, he quickly realized, but he didn't offer to help at once. Instead, he watched as she put her back into each swing, giving her bottom a provocative little wiggle in the process.

Her jacket lay in a heap on the snow. Thanks to the light of day, he had a better view of her than he'd had last night and so he took in the fit of her jeans and turtleneck shirt. No secrets today, he realized, relishing the full feminine curves her clothing revealed. Suddenly, Ryan felt the strongest urge to walk up behind Dani and press his body close.

He closed his eyes and imagined slipping his hands under her shirt and bra so he could cup his fingers around her bare breasts. Her skin would feel smooth as silk, he guessed, and her nipples soft...until he teased them to tautness, that is. Moving those same hands down her midriff in further exploration, he'd naturally encounter the barrier of her jeans.

But what kind of barrier was a zipper or a snap to a man on fire?

"Hey, over there! Are you sleepwalking or what?"

With a guilty jolt, Ryan came to life and found that Dani had spotted him hiding behind the sapling just a few feet away. He felt his face glow crimson and could only hope that she didn't notice the other physical evidence of his shocking, ill-timed fantasy, which now tested the buttons of his fly.

"Actually," he said as he walked over to her, "I came out here for the same reason you did—to find a Christmas tree."

"Were you going to pick it like a daisy?" She directed her gaze to his empty hands.

"Of course not. I heard someone out here and guessed it might be you. Naturally, I came to help."

"So help," she said, handing him the ax.

Immediately, Ryan tested the edge of the blade. "I could probably gnaw that tree down faster than this blade will ever cut it."

Dani sighed. "The grinder is in the shed. Sharpening this ax can be your very first task as my *temporary* ranch hand."

"Actually, making the coffee was my first task," he retorted, adding, "Why don't you go in and have a cup? You look as if you could use it." In truth, her cheeks glowed scarlet with cold, and he noticed that her teeth had begun to chatter. Scooping up her jacket, probably shed for ease of movement, he held it out so she could slip into it.

Dani did, then gave him a smile. "I'm not the most wonderful cook in the world, but I'm pretty good with pancakes. Is that okay for breakfast?"

"Cook anything you like," Ryan said. "We'll never complain."

They walked together as far as the toolshed, both silent. She did not stop since the door had been left ajar, but nodded a goodbye as Ryan veered off to duck into the building. He found the grinder, mounted on a sturdy wooden worktable, without any trouble.

While Ryan sharpened the ax blade, he tried to analyze the reasons for what had happened in the woods, from the sudden onset of his lustful fantasy, to its embarrassing physical result. Such an analysis proved next to impossible since Dani wasn't the sort of woman who normally turned him on. As a rule, he preferred taller females, probably because of his own six-three height. Critical body parts—private parts—fit together best when the woman stood nearly heads even. Besides that, he favored brunettes, though, now that he thought about it, he hadn't had much luck with them so far.

Maybe it *was* time for a blonde.

Time for a blonde? Ryan nearly dropped the ax. It wasn't time for a blonde. It wasn't time for any woman. He had a son now, an impressionable son who needed food and clothing, a son whose upbringing would require dedication and full concentration. The last thing Ryan needed was the distraction of some female. Not that Dani could ever really distract him. She couldn't. Clearly, the problem was him. Deprived of the pleasures of sex for too long now, his libido was just a little trigger-happy.

Trigger-happy.

Ryan laughed aloud at that unfortunate metaphor. So his libido was trigger-happy, huh? Well, something told him he'd damn well better keep it holstered lest it get him kicked off Dani's ranch. She had a chip on her shoulder the size of Pike's Peak, and it didn't take a genius to figure out that a man—maybe even a cowboy—had put it there.

When the blade of the ax felt sharp to Ryan's touch, he switched off the grinder and turned to head back outdoors, but paused first, giving the room a cursory examination. He saw a mess—clutter that could only result from years of neglect. Ryan, who despised a disorderly workroom such as this one, placed the cleaning of it high on a mental list of tasks he intended to accomplish over the next few days.

Just before he stepped through the door, he spied a basket, one of the kind so often sold at craft fairs for use as decoration. Ryan paused again, then impulsively scooped up the basket, which looked fairly new, by its handle. He could make use of it to remedy a situation that had bothered him all night.

Ax and basket in hand, he walked back to the pine tree Dani had picked out and quickly chopped it down. He left the tree where it lay for a few minutes while he searched for pinecones, easily visible in the sparse snow beneath some of the larger pine trees several yards away. There were plenty to choose from, ranging from small to huge. Ryan picked up quite a few and put them into Dani's basket, which looked pretty dusty now that he had it out in good light.

Ryan tried to remember if he'd seen an outside water spigot. He couldn't, and had almost decided he'd have to carry the basket indoors, thus spoiling what he'd intended to be a surprise, when he heard the unmistakable trickle of water. He froze, straining to hear the sound again. When he heard it a second later, Ryan followed it into the woods, where he soon stumbled onto a spring.

He wished for his camera to capture forever the beauty of the winter scene—snowbanks, trickling stream, gnarled tree roots at his feet, a canopy of tangled bare limbs over his head. Enchanted, Ryan knelt and dipped his hand into the ice-cold water, then raised it to his lips so he could sip. He grinned. Delicious!

Next, he proceeded to wipe down the basket with his hands, which were now red and rough from the cold. When it passed inspection, he set it down so he could gather some of the colorful pebbles lying all around. They were smooth and round, thanks to time and water flow. He laid them inside the basket with the pinecones.

He gathered other natural artifacts, all of which he tucked into the basket. In his mind's eye, he arranged and rearranged everything. By the time he walked back to get the tree, he had a good idea what he wanted to do.

Leaving the basket sitting behind a wooden chair on the side porch and placing the tree near the door, Ryan stomped the snow off his boots and stepped into the kitchen. On the floor just inside the door, a Christmas-tree stand waited.

"Finally!" Dani exclaimed from where she stood frying bacon at the stove. Her smile said she wasn't scolding, just impatient to get started decorating the tree.

Ryan noted that Sawyer had risen and dressed and was now helping Dani by setting the table. The boy did a good job, arranging the colorful plates on coordinating place mats and placing napkins and silverware to the side while she instructed.

"Actually," Dani said, "I don't know why I'm so anxious about the tree. We can't decorate it until after breakfast, and that won't be ready for another ten minutes."

"Then I think I'll go ahead and get the tree set up in the living room," Ryan told her, lifting the stand and heading outside. Several minutes after, he reentered the house via the front door and proceeded to situate the tree in the stand. That accomplished, he stepped back to examine it. Dani had chosen well, he realized, noting the symmetry of the branches.

"It's ready!" she called out.

Ryan returned to the kitchen and washed his hands, then joined them at the small, wooden kitchen table. Dani held out one hand to him across the food. The other she held out to Sawyer, seated to her right, an action that baffled Ryan until he remembered the old custom of joining hands to return grace. Somewhat awkwardly, he took her hand and extended his other one to Sawyer. Taking his cue from his dad, Sawyer quickly completed the link. Dani bowed her head, and in a clear, sweet voice, thanked her maker for their food, their shelter and each other.

She tried to release his hand immediately after her soft "amen," but Ryan wouldn't allow it. Instead, he tightened his grip slightly, a move that earned him a questioning look.

"I want you to know how grateful I, uh, *we* are to be here. You didn't have to take us in."

"It's no big deal," she said, clearly uncomfortable with his thanks.

"Maybe not to you," he said. "It is to me. And I'll never forget it." That said, he released her.

Cheeks stained an attractive pink that had nothing to do with the cold, Dani could only stare at him for a moment before coming to life and thrusting a plate stacked with pancakes in his direction.

Ryan took the food, but instead of helping himself, he offered the pancakes to Sawyer, who forked a stack, the next instant exclaiming, "Look! Christmas trees."

Christmas trees? Belatedly, Ryan realized to what Sawyer referred—the pancakes. Somehow, Dani had shaped each like a Christmas tree and decorated it with blueberries. And she said she couldn't cook....

"Some of them are a little lopsided," she said, shrugging self-consciously.

"I like 'em just fine!" Sawyer gleefully assured her. His grin stretched from ear to ear.

Oddly pleased that she'd taken such pains to make Sawyer's Christmas breakfast so special, Ryan helped himself to a short stack of the "trees," then passed the plate back to

Dani. Butter and syrup came next, then the bacon. Soon everyone ate in contented silence.

"I like this," Sawyer suddenly announced.

"Pancakes are my favorite, too," Dani said.

"I'm not talking about them," Sawyer told her. "I'm talking about us eating together. It's just like at my friend Robby's house. He sits at the table every single morning with his mom and dad and eats stuff like this."

His mom and dad? Ryan nearly choked at the comparison.

Dani, however, looked amused. "And what do you usually do for breakfast?"

"Well, when I lived with Granny Wright in Arkansas, I always had cereal and milk," Sawyer told her around a huge bite of pancake. Ryan bit back the urge to tell him not to talk with his mouth full. "Dad and I have doughnuts and cookies and stuff."

Ryan felt Dani's accusing gaze on him and squirmed in the chair. "That's because you told me you didn't eat cereal," he said. "You know I don't have time to cook in the mornings."

"It's okay, Dad," Sawyer hastily assured Ryan, as if afraid he might have hurt his feelings. "I like what we have."

Dani said nothing—at least not out loud. But her expression spoke volumes, and Ryan saw curiosity and speculation in her eyes. At once, he made two mental vows, the first to keep his personal business to himself. As for the second, well, that was to drag his butt out of bed a little earlier from now on to cook his kid some eggs or something.

"Tell me about your Granny Wright," Dani said to Sawyer. "How long did you live with her?"

"Until she died."

Ryan bit back a smile at Sawyer's innocent answer, which didn't begin to answer Dani's question.

"I'm sorry about your grandmother, Sawyer. I'm sure you miss her." Dani took a sip of coffee, then tried again. "Where did you stay until your dad came to get you?"

"At Granny Wright's house with Erica."

"Erica?"

"My mom."

"Your mom?" The words were a squeak of surprise. As though aware she sounded like a parrot, Dani hastily explained, "I'd assumed she was dead or something."

Sawyer giggled as only an eight-year-old boy can. "No way." He said nothing else, but went on shoveling pancakes into his mouth, an action that left Dani visibly frustrated.

Apparently giving up on getting information from the boy, she raised her gaze to Ryan. "You and Sawyer's mother are divorced?"

Ryan shook his head. "We never married."

"I...see," Dani murmured, even though she couldn't possibly. Clearly, her curiosity battled the need to protect Sawyer from whatever truth Ryan so obviously resisted sharing.

"Erica's a movie star," Sawyer offered as he reached for his glass of milk. "She don't have time to take care of a kid." He spoke the words as if he was quoting them...no evidence of blame or pain, just a flat statement of fact that stabbed Ryan's heart.

Dani caught her breath, a soft sound Sawyer didn't appear to hear. Without uttering a word, she rose suddenly from the table and walked over to the counter to stand for several seconds with her back to them. Sawyer went right on eating.

Ryan barely acknowledged Dani's action, himself, since familiar fury roiled inside him, hot as a volcano about to blow. He'd felt it before, this all-consuming rage, this bitterness, and realized that it seemed to be getting hotter, more intense with each passing day. How long until eruption? he wondered. How long until he lost control and verbalized truths that his son did not need to hear about Erica, the "movie star" who didn't want to be called *mom* because it made her feel old?

"What's your favorite thing about Christmas, Dad?" Sawyer suddenly asked, an innocent subject change that forced Ryan to ignore the pain in his heart.

He had to suck in a deep, calming breath before he could answer. "Um, cookies, I guess. My aunt Mabel used to make the best Santa-shaped ones. They had this red icing on them and these little sparkle things, all colors." He faked a smile. "Er, Dani, what's your favorite thing about Christmas?"

Slowly, she turned and walked back to the table. She didn't sit, but reached for her plate. Holding it as though she'd lost her appetite and couldn't bear to look at the food, she said after a moment, "I'd have to say the tree."

Ryan noted that her eyes shimmered suspiciously. Tears? Almost certainly, and a sure indication of a very soft heart. Since he'd never met a woman with one of those before, he didn't quite know what to make of it or what to do about it.

Oblivious to Ryan's bemusement, Dani smiled at Sawyer. "What about you? What's your favorite thing?"

"This Christmas it's *every*thing!" Sawyer exclaimed, throwing out his arms as if to encompass all the magic of the season.

Dani laughed then, a light, happy sound that did much to cool Ryan's rage at Sawyer's mother. "Why don't we leave all these dishes for now and get busy on the tree? I don't think I can wait another minute!"

"All right!" Sawyer said excitedly, slipping from his chair and dashing out of the room. Ryan stood, too, and slowly walked toward the door.

Dani caught his arm, stopping him. "Just tell me this, and I won't ask another question. Before last September, did you know you had a son?"

He met her probing gaze without a blink. "I did not."

"Somehow I knew that." Dani sighed and stepped close to slip one arm around his waist, gently hugging him to her side. "And I'm so sorry."

Astonished by the unexpected display of sympathy, Ryan could do nothing more than return the embrace somewhat awkwardly by laying his arm over her back and shoulders. She hugged him harder in response. Almost instantly, Ryan felt the tension begin to drain from his body. Several seconds passed before Dani released him from the healing half hug and stepped away, tears on her cheeks.

"You saw the ornaments in the living room?" she asked, unselfconsciously swiping the drops away with her fingers.

He nodded.

"Then why don't you go help your son get started. I'm going to pour myself another cup of coffee. Want one?"

"Sure."

With a nod, she retrieved their mugs from the table and walked over to the stove. She poured one mugful, then turned to glance curiously at Ryan, still rooted to the spot near the door. "Something wrong?"

"Actually, I think something's right," he murmured—words straight from the heart and, therefore, uncensored. Words that seemed to surprise her as much as they did him. Embarrassed, he turned abruptly on his heel and left the room.

Only later, when the three of them worked at hanging colorful glass balls, homemade wooden stars and glittering icicles on the tree, did Ryan think about what he'd said to her in the kitchen.

Something *was* right at this moment. Or maybe a lot of somethings, now that he thought about it. For the first time in his young life, Sawyer was having a fun Christmas, something Erica's stern, no-frills mother would never have tolerated. Ryan, himself, was seeing the holiday season through Sawyer's eyes—a joyful, renewing experience he cherished.

And Dani... well, who knew about his mystery employer? From all appearances, she enjoyed having the two of them around to share her Christmas. Ryan couldn't imagine why, since it was bound to mean more work for her. He silently vowed to make her efforts worthwhile by working his butt off for her until he hit the road. From the looks of the ranch, there was much to be done in the way of cleanup and repair, not to mention caring for the livestock.

On that thought, Ryan suddenly remembered the horses she boarded. "Do I need to feed and water the horses?"

"No ranch work on Christmas," she told him, adding, "I put out extra feed yesterday," as she hung a reindeer with a tiny light bulb for a nose on the tree. She threaded the green electrical cord attached to it up the branch then down the trunk, where she plugged it into the extension cord that would provide electricity to the rest of the twinkling tree lights when connected to the electrical outlet on the wall. Smiling with pleasure, Dani turned to Sawyer. "See Rudolph, here?"

The boy nodded.

"I won him at a school carnival when I was your age."

"They had electricity then?"

His grin gave away the fact that he was joking, but Dani squealed and pounced on him all the same. They fell to the floor in a heap, both laughing hysterically as she paid him back for his teasing insult with torturous tickles.

"Save me, Dad! Save me!" Sawyer gasped.

Who could resist such a plea? Not Ryan, who instantly reached down and plucked Dani off his squirming son. She countered the move by reaching back to goose him in the ribs. With a yelp, he instinctively wrapped his arms around her, immobilizing the attack and putting her exactly where he'd put her in his delicious fantasy—back to front with him.

The all-woman scent of her assailed him. Her breasts, crushed under his arms, tantalized beyond endurance, as did her derriere, brushing his manly front every time she struggled to be free. With a soft *oomph!* of pure sexual overload, Ryan released her as abruptly as he'd captured her.

Clearly unaware of the state of his libido, unholstered again in spite of all his good intentions, Dani turned. "What's wrong?" she demanded between pants for air.

"You stepped on my foot," he lied.

Breathless, flushed, beautiful—yes, God help him, beautiful—she eyed his foot with visible regret. "Oh. I'm sorry. That's what I get for fooling around when I should be decorating the tree."

Fooling around? Ryan, who could think of nothing he'd enjoy more, gulped audibly and had to look away. Though he actually ached with the need to be lying face-to-face with Dani in a bed somewhere private—bodies bare, legs tangled, hearts afire—he nonetheless feared her.

Warmhearted, caring, she had the innate potential to wreak havoc on his and Sawyer's future by setting precedents impossible to maintain. And, inevitably, whatever life he made with his son would suffer by comparison.

Chapter Three

"Tell me about *this* ornament," Sawyer said. He held up a decoration shaped like a candy cane and sporting angled red-and-white stripes.

"My mother and I made that from salt dough when I was about your age," Dani told him.

"Where's your mother now?"

The question, uttered in innocence, brought back painful memories of arguments, partings, regrets. "She died years ago."

"Do you miss her?" Sawyer asked as he draped an icicle over a branch.

Ryan shook his head at his son, clearly trying to discourage further questions. With a wave of her hand, Dani told him it was okay. "Sometimes."

"Can I put the star on the top of the tree?" the boy asked.

"Sure," Dani murmured, amazed by the agility of the eight-year-old mind, which could leap from death to tinsel stars in the blink of an eye. "Want the ladder, or can your dad lift you up there?"

"Dad can do it," Sawyer said. Ryan obliged, a move that demonstrated impressive upper body strength and made Dani long to be captured in those powerful arms again.

Quite a sensation, that. Her heart rate still hadn't slowed to normal.

"Ready to turn on the lights?" she asked.

"Yes!" Sawyer exclaimed.

Ryan did the honors, plugging the cord into the socket even as Dani turned off the overhead light. At once the tree twinkled red, blue, green and yellow. Sawyer whooped his delight and made it a point to see if Rudolph's nose glowed red. It did.

"Do you suppose it's too late for old Santa to find us?" Dani asked.

Sawyer's smile faded just a little. "Probably, but that's okay. We'll have lots of presents next year in Wyoming, won't we, Dad?"

"Sure thing," Ryan agreed, exchanging a glance with Dani.

Later? she asked without words, hoping Ryan would allow her to surprise the boy by slipping the present under the tree sometime during the day. Ryan nodded as if he instinctively understood her plan.

Pleased, Dani excused herself to the kitchen, leaving the men to clean up what mess had been made and stash the decoration box in the toolshed. A woman with a plan, she made short work of clearing the breakfast things. She then mixed up sugar cookie dough, which she set in the refrigerator to chill, all the while keeping out an ear and an eye for the pair.

The sounds of their voices out back reassured her. Busy with who knew what, they laughed, talked and argued good-naturedly for the better part of the morning, during which she baked three dozen cookies, all shaped like Santa Claus and decorated with red icing and sprinkles. She didn't examine her motives for trying to give Ryan something he'd said he loved for Christmas. It was enough that she could do this little thing for him. While the cookies baked, she stewed a hen for dinner, just as her mother and grandmother had always done on this special day. Christmas without hen and dressing would not be Christmas at all.

Just as she tucked the last cookie into a decorated tin, Sawyer burst into the room. "Do you have any construction paper?" he asked.

"Look in the bottom right-hand drawer of the desk in my office," Dani told him, wisely not asking why he needed them.

"And scissors?"

"Middle drawer of the desk."

"And glue?"

"Top left." Still, she didn't ask a single question. Sawyer rewarded her for her reticence with a smile as bright as the lights on their tree, then charged from the room.

I could get used to having this kid around, Dani realized, a thought that made her sad. Ruefully, she acknowledged that inviting Ryan and his son into her home probably wasn't the smartest thing she'd ever done. By nature a people person, Dani had struggled hard to gain independence the last few years. Three days with these guys could well result in a crash landing back on square one and a resurrection of dreams long dead.

Was it worth it, just to have company for Christmas? Dani wondered. Nowhere near knowing the answer to that question, she peeked into the hall trying to locate Ryan and Sawyer. Since she heard their voices in the office, she felt safe to slip the tin of cookies and the remote-control car, originally purchased for Ricky, under the tree.

Then, suddenly inspired, she headed to her bedroom at the back of the house. In the walk-in closet, a ladder led to the attic. Armed with the flashlight she always kept by her bed, Dani climbed up into the spacious storage area. There, she perused an old bookshelf loaded down with board games, books and other toys saved from childhood—further evidence of her "sentimental softie" tendencies.

Armed with a like-new Monopoly game and a shoe box full of baseball cards—she'd been a tomboy from the get go—Dani descended the ladder again. Cleaning up the boxes took seconds, after which she wrapped them in colorful paper and added them to the stash under the tree.

The rest of the day passed in a pleasant blur of activity. They snacked on cheese and saltines for lunch, watched *Miracle on 34th Street* and *A Christmas Story,* then drank hot chocolate while they stood on the front porch and exclaimed over the silver-dollar-size snowflakes that began to drift to the ground around 4:00 p.m.

One eye ever on the Christmas tree and the packages that kept appearing so mysteriously under it, Sawyer fairly bounced off the walls in anticipation of the special dinner Dani had promised, not to mention the thought of opening his presents.

At last, dinnertime rolled around. When they finally laid down their forks and moved into the living room, all three of them were stuffed with hen and dressing. Dani, by now a little tired, settled into her favorite recliner and let Ryan run the show. He did so by allowing Sawyer to play Santa Claus and pass out the presents, the total of which had somehow multiplied again, this time without her help.

Her jaw dropped in surprise when Sawyer handed her a homemade Christmas card and something else, rather large, roundish and wrapped in newspaper.

"Open it," Sawyer ordered, pointing to the present and clearly impatient.

Dani did and laughed her delight at the sight of a basket filled with gifts from nature. Artfully arranged on a bed of moss, she found pinecones and needles of various sizes, and a bird nest, in which lay three egg-shaped pebbles, each a different color. A sprig of mistletoe, adorned with waxlike berries of white, and a strategic twist of vine covered the handle, completing the array.

She raised her gaze to Ryan, startled that the cowboy had such an eye for beauty. "I don't know what to say. It's incredible."

"Glad you like it," he murmured, clearly embarrassed.

"This is mistlefinger," Sawyer said, pointing to the basket handle.

"*Toe.* Mistle*toe,*" his dad corrected, laughing heartily. He turned to Dani. "Can you believe this son of mine had never seen mistletoe before? I had to demonstrate where to hang it and then explain why."

"You have to kiss any girl you find standing under it," Sawyer informed Dani. He then crossed his eyes and stuck out his tongue, demonstrating exactly what he thought of *that.*

"He's young yet," Dani said to Ryan, who could only stare at his son in horror.

Sawyer, clearly tired of the topic, thrust a Christmas tin at Ryan and ordered him to open it. After double-checking that the present was, indeed, for him, Ryan flashed a look of surprise at Dani.

"All right!" he exclaimed the moment he pried off the lid. He tasted one of the cookies and sighed his pleasure.

"Just like Aunt Mabel's. I thought you said you weren't the most wonderful cook in the world."

"I'm not."

"Could've fooled me," he said, words that made Dani blush.

"Time to open your presents," she quickly prompted Sawyer, now helping himself to one of his dad's cookies.

"What about your card?" the boy asked, almost as if postponing the moment when he finally got to open his presents.

"Oops. I forgot." Obediently, Dani tore open the white construction paper card, now decorated with a cut-up poinsettia, and read the carefully penned message inside.

Poinsettias are red.
Ornaments are blue.
Christmas is special
Because we're with you.

Thanks from
Ryan and Sawyer

At once a lump rose in Dani's throat. With difficulty, she swallowed it and managed a smile. "Did you compose this yourself?" she asked the child hovering at her elbow.

He nodded.

"Well, you're very talented," she exclaimed, adding, "I had no idea I had a poet under my roof," before hugging him.

Though Sawyer stiffened at her initial touch, just as his father had that morning, he relaxed within seconds. Dani marveled that instead of returning the embrace, the boy patted her arm, much as a parent might do when comforting offspring. Clearly, this child wasn't used to being hugged, which explained the lack of physical affection between him and Ryan that she'd already wondered about.

"Thanks a million . . . both of you." She included Ryan, who watched with an undecipherable expression on his face. "Now, Sawyer, open your presents before I die of impatience!"

Sawyer didn't need to be told twice. He ripped into the packages, exclaiming over each of them. Dani had no trouble reading the expression on Ryan's face now. She saw pleasure. She saw surprise. She saw love. She also saw little-boy excitement that matched Sawyer's when the child opened the shoe box packed with old baseball cards.

"Good grief, Dani!" Ryan exclaimed when they began to sort through them. "You've got a 1975 George Brett rookie card in here that's surely worth a hundred and fifty bucks."

"Only if you sell it," she teased. "Are you going to?"

Clearly aghast, Ryan exclaimed, "Not no, but he—er, *heck* no!"

"We're keeping it forever," Sawyer assured her, hugging the card to his heart.

For the better part of the evening and into the night, Ryan and Sawyer sifted through the cards, both totally engrossed. Congratulating herself for remembering them in the first place, Dani escaped to the kitchen around nine o'clock for a few moments alone. Her visitors were as addictive as a drug, providing a constant high she found as exhausting as it was exhilarating. Now, she needed time out.

Dani turned on her old radio and searched for a station that wasn't playing Christmas music. Finally she heard a staticy country rock song that had nothing to do with the season. As she wiped down the kitchen table, she danced to the music, an attempt to release some of the tension accumulated during the day.

In seconds Dani felt better. When the music died, she turned to the sink and found herself face-to-face with Ryan, who reached out and tugged her into his arms.

"How long have you been standing there?" she blurted out, even as a country ballad began to play, its beat a seductive *one*, two, three. *One*, two, three.

Ryan did not answer, but in perfect time with the music swept her around the room. Dani, who hadn't danced with a partner in years, struggled to match his steps, her gaze locked with his as they moved.

Though proper execution of the dance demanded that there be space between them, Ryan pulled her so close that she stood on tiptoe. She felt the thump of his heart, fast and furious against hers. He moved with surprising grace for such a large man, and politely ignored her stumbles.

The music faded, then died. Dani, by now highly aware of more than just Ryan's rapid heart rate, stood in stunned silence in his arms, trying to deal with some unexpected truths.

The man wanted her. Sexually. Now.

Desire surged through her veins in response to the knowledge—dizzying, potent. Her body tensed with need. Undeniably, unforgivably, she wanted him, too. The sudden gleam in his eye said he knew it.

"Ryan, I—"

"Dani, I—"

"Hey, Dad, will you bring me a glass of milk?"

Fortunately, Sawyer called the question from the living room. Coiled tight as a spring inside, Dani broke free of Ryan's embrace and fumbled to get a glass from the cabinet. He came to her aid at once, located one and then poured milk into it from a jug he removed from the refrigerator. Dani noticed that his hands did not shake as hers did. That, more than anything, sobered her.

The moment Ryan left the room with the glass of milk, Dani escaped out the kitchen door and into the winter night. Snow still fell and a chill breeze gusted. She sat on one of the wooden chairs on the side porch and watched the flakes swirl around the security lights, her arms crossed over her breasts in an automatic self-hug she sorely needed.

"Dani?" Ryan was back in the kitchen now and looking for her, probably to finish what he'd so expertly started.

Ah, heaven save her from another cowboy. Mysterious as Zorro, debonair as Don Juan, appealing as Roy Rogers—he was each and every little-girl fantasy come to life and awakening some very grown-up needs.

Dani felt the wooden planks beneath her feet tremble every time Ryan took a step, and knew without looking when he reached the back door and stepped out into the night.

"What are you doing out here?" he asked.

"Cooling off."

"I can help you do that." His voice, sexy as silk, tantalized and tempted her.

Dani swallowed hard. Her reply came out a panicky whisper. "No you can't."

"Why not?" He stood right beside her now, little more than a silhouette asking a question she could not begin to answer just then, when her body believed there *was* no good reason.

"In case you've forgotten, there's a little boy inside the house."

"Little boys sleep, Dani. We'll wait him out and—"

"No."

"So there's another reason you're hiding out here?" He didn't sound surprised.

"Yes, there is... a good one. I don't intend to have a relationship with you while you're here."

"And who said anything about a relationship?" He dropped to one knee by the chair, which put his face nearly level with Dani's, leaving her no choice but to meet his gaze—so intense, so piercing. "I'm talking about sex, here. Simple no-strings sex between two lonely people who happen to be incredibly attracted to one another."

She laughed to hide her discomfiture at his honesty and use of the word *lonely.* Was it so obvious that she'd been on her own too long? And was he really lonely, too, or just making the most of her vulnerability? "No-strings sex? You mean, you really think there's such a thing?"

Long silence followed the question—silence during which Ryan surprised her by slowly standing and walking to the porch railing.

"No, I guess I don't," he finally murmured as he kicked a drift of snow off the porch and then gazed out over the yard. This was *not* the answer Dani had expected.

"Then you understand why I can't sleep with you now...or ever?"

"Ever?" *He* laughed this time, but without humor, and looked back at her. "That's a hell of a long time from now, lady. How can you be so sure you won't change your mind?"

"Because I know what I want, and it isn't sex with a stranger."

"We've introduced ourselves, shared a roof plus several meals and exchanged Christmas gifts. I'm no stranger."

He had a point. "Then let me rephrase that. I know what I want, and it isn't sex with a *cowboy.*"

She might as well have said bum, or idiot, or deviant, judging by Ryan's reaction. He flinched as if she'd slapped him—and, in a way, she had. Dani instantly regretted her insulting tone.

"I didn't mean that the way it sounded," she blurted out.

"Yes, you did," he said, the next instant stepping back into the house.

"Damn!" Dani exclaimed, breaking her own rule about cursing. She sprang to her feet and followed Ryan, who was already halfway down the hall. "Wait! I owe you an explanation."

"This *cowboy* don't need one, ma'am." His voice dripped with sarcasm and twanged with a phony Texas drawl.

"But you don't understand—"

"Yes, I do. Now, don't worry yore pretty li'l head about this. I know my place, and I'll stay in it." With that, he disappeared into his room, shutting the door firmly behind him.

Sick at heart and half-angry with him for the *pretty li'l head* comment, Dani stalked into the living room, where Sawyer still sat on the floor, guiding his buzzing race car around the room. She sat in the recliner, then tucked her feet up under her, unwilling to have her toes involved in a hit and run.

Questions spun around inside her head, questions about Ryan—his past, his present, his future. She would ask Sawyer, she decided. Even though he'd met his dad only a few months ago, it was worth a try.

"I'm curious about your mother...I mean, Erica," Dani said, trying to begin at the beginning. "Does it bother you to talk about her?"

Sawyer, remote control in hand, shook his head without shifting his attention from his rolling car.

"Where does she live?"

"California." *Buzz, buzz.* "She has a big house with a swimming pool and everything."

"You've been there?"

"Nah, but I have a picture of it." With a sigh of impatience, he lay down the remote control and dug into the pocket of his blue jeans. Extracting a tooled-leather wallet, he withdrew two color photographs which had been folded to fit in it.

Dani took the one he handed her, badly creased though it was, and examined it. She saw a lovely brunette, dressed in a tiny bikini and seated on a lawn chair near an oval pool. It looked like a publicity shot of some kind. "Has your mom been in a lot of movies?" she asked, giving him back the picture.

"I guess." He tucked the photos back into his wallet, then put it into his pocket and picked up the remote control again. "Dad told me he met her when she was making one in Texas." *Buzz, buzz.*

"She's very beautiful."

"She's okay," Sawyer said with a shrug, annihilating Dani's just-formulated theory that the child idolized his absent mother.

"Are you disappointed that she didn't take you to California after your Granny Wright died?"

"I was at first," Sawyer admitted. "But then Dad came, and I was real glad. He's pretty neat."

"I agree," Dani murmured, adding, "I don't think you could find a better dad if you got to pick one out yourself, do you?"

"Uh-uh." *Buzz, buzz.*

"So tell me about him."

"What do you want to know?"

"Well . . . has he always worked on a ranch?"

"If you're curious about my qualifications, why don't you just ask me?"

Dani whirled at the sound of Ryan's voice, so close behind her, when she'd left him down the hall. "I thought you were sulking in your room."

He had the grace to look embarrassed. "I'm not now," he murmured, walking over to sit on the couch, near her chair.

With a quick glance at Sawyer, who appeared engrossed in his car, Dani shifted her position so that she leaned toward Ryan. "I apologize for what I said out on the porch," she told him, her voice low. "You must think I'm a first-class snob."

"I expect you had your reasons," Ryan replied. "And I had mine for overreacting, which is why I'm in here...to explain." He sat without speaking for a moment, then shrugged. "Let's just say that your words triggered an old memory, and leave it at that."

"An old memory...." Dani laughed without humor. "Would you believe an old memory is exactly what made me lash out at you the way I did? I'm really not prejudiced against cowboys, Ryan, most of them, anyway. But there is one I'd love to kick all the way to Tombstone." She picked at a piece of invisible lint on the arm of her corduroy chair.

"Give me the varmint's name, and I'll do it for you," Ryan said.

He sounded so sincere that Dani's gaze flew back up at him. "For a minute there, I thought you meant it."

"I do mean it."

Dani laughed again, this time in honest amusement. "Actually, he's not worth the effort, and he's so long gone, we'd probably never find him, anyway."

"Are we talking about some guy who used to work for you?"

"We're talking about my ex-husband, Mick Harrison." She gave Ryan a wan smile. "A cowboy from the top of his hat to the toes of his boots. So you see, I'm not a snob at all."

Ryan nodded. "I also see that there's not much chance of your getting close to another wrangler."

"I did learn a hard lesson."

"He hurt you?"

"In more ways than I can say, but I'm over it now."

When Ryan arched an eyebrow, clearly questioning the truth of her statement, Dani felt her cheeks go hot. With a quick glance toward Sawyer, now following his car down the hall, Dani said, "Let's just leave it at that—I'm as much over him as you are over whoever said she wasn't interested in sex with a cowboy."

"That would be Erica."

Dani's jaw dropped. "Excuse me, but as I understand the birds and bees thing, sex generally precedes pregnancy."

"Hmm. Well, perhaps I didn't quote her exactly. Perhaps she really said that she wasn't interested in *marrying* a cowboy."

Dani noted his grim expression. This was a wound that time had not yet healed, she realized.

"I was working in Texas," he continued. "On a three-thousand-acre ranch. This two-bit Hollywood movie company came around, wanting to film on location, and my boss agreed."

"Sawyer told me you met his mother while she was making a movie."

"That's right. We were pretty thick while she was there—"

"One word for it."

Ryan winced and gave her a rueful grin. "Yeah, well, when I heard from a mutual friend that she was pregnant, I assumed I was responsible, and I proposed. You already know how that turned out."

Dani frowned. "But I thought you said you didn't learn about Sawyer until last September?"

"Erica told me the baby's father was the movie director, not me. I now know that she was trying to trick the guy into marrying her. For a while, it looked as if her little scheme was working, then he ditched her. By then, it was too late for an abortion. She went home to her mother's place in Arkansas, had the baby, then split . . . without him."

"Her mother must have been a saint."

"Her mother was a fundamentalist fanatic," he said, his voice cold. "And if I'd known that she had my son—" He broke off, shaking his head.

"Sawyer seems well-adjusted," Dani ventured.

"He does, doesn't he?" Ryan sounded relieved.

For a second neither of them spoke. That was long enough for Dani to marvel that she'd just shared her most intimate secrets with a virtual stranger and had heard some of his in return.

"That's about all the true confessions I can stand," Ryan drawled, getting to his feet. He appeared a little flushed. Dani guessed he felt as awkward about their tête-à-tête as she did. "Sawyer?" he called down the hall. "You going to play with that car all night?"

"Can I?"

Ryan laughed and winked at Dani. "If you promise to haul your butt out of bed and help me out around the ranch tomorrow. We'll start about sunup."

The *buzz, buzz* instantly ceased. Dani heard the clump of Sawyer's cowboy boots—miniatures of his dad's—on the hardwood floor as he walked back to the living room.

"Guess I'd better go to bed now, huh?"

"Guess you'd better," Ryan solemnly agreed.

With a heartfelt sigh, Sawyer walked up to Dani's chair. "This was the best Christmas ever."

"I think so, too," Dani said, rising to hug him. Sawyer did not retreat this time, but tolerated the hug with aplomb. "Now hug your dad good-night."

Ryan started noticeably, and then, as if trying to cover his reaction, stood and reached out an arm to his son. Sawyer hurled himself at his dad. They hugged for long moments—so long that Dani silently confirmed what she'd guessed: This was a first. Tears stung her eyes.

"Now, off to bed," Ryan said, his voice undeniably husky with emotion. He swatted Sawyer on the rear and sent him down the hall to his bedroom, which doubled as a sewing room. That left Dani and Ryan alone by the Christmas tree.

"I want to know what we're going to do about what happened on the porch," he murmured, most likely an attempt to discourage discussion about the hug.

"You mean, my insulting you?" Dani said softly, graciously following his lead.

Ryan shook his head. "We settled that already. I'm talking about this thing between us . . . this physical attraction. I want to know where we go from here."

"Why, nowhere," she blurted out, taken aback by his frank words. Hadn't he gotten the picture yet?

"Oh." He sounded as disappointed as she felt.

Their gazes locked. How long had it been since she'd read such obvious want in a man's face? Dani wondered. It flattered. It flustered. It tempted . . . oh, how it tempted. Turning away from his heated stare, she began to click out the lights, but her thoughts weren't on the task.

They were on no-strings, no-consequences, no-worry sex.

Sheer physical thrill. Intense mutual gratification. A few hours' comfort and communication. The best Christmas present ever.

An impossible dream? Now dizzy with wanting him, Dani naturally thought not. Unlike Mick, this cowboy had money of his own, so he did not have designs on hers, if, in fact, he knew about it. Dani doubted that he did. Once bitten, twice shy, she'd deliberately not told him the size of her ranch—one thousand acres.

So why not give each other a few Christmas memories? Why not share a night—or three—of hot—but safe—sex.

Dani's heart began to thump at the mere idea of having a man in her bed again. She half feared that Ryan could hear it as they headed down the hall together.

"What time do you start your day?" he asked when they reached her bedroom door.

"Five o'clock, but only because I have to get my chores done before I can work on the wedding dress. Six should be okay for tomorrow. I'll show you where everything is, then leave you to it." She marveled that she could sound so normal when her heart beat so wildly.

"Or I could find it all on my own. I'm really pretty handy around a ranch."

And in the bedroom, I'll bet, Dani thought, the next instant giving herself a mental get-it-together! shake. But who could resist a cowboy so fetching? Not Dani, with her documented weakness for them.

Weakness?

Yes, weakness *was* the culprit here, she suddenly realized. Weakness for the look, smell, feel of him. And there were other character flaws to blame besides weakness—loneliness, and foolish optimism, among them. There was no such thing as safe sex, and she knew it. Besides, there was Sawyer to think of.

Without a doubt, she'd be an idiot to get sexually involved with Ryan Given. No good could possibly come of it. She couldn't believe she'd considered such craziness for even a second.

"Good night, Dani."

"Good night." She stepped deliberately into her room, intending to shut the door firmly behind her. When she turned to do it, however, she found that Ryan had not moved down the hall, but now stood right in her doorway.

"I forgot to tell you again how grateful I am for what you did for us today," he said, his blue eyes solemn. "Sawyer will never forget it, and neither will I. What would have been the worst Christmas of our lives was the best, thanks to you."

Struck speechless by his eloquent words, Dani barely managed a nod of acknowledgment. It was then that she spied the mistletoe, taped to the door frame right over Ryan's head. So this was where he'd demonstrated where to hang mistletoe to his son—an interesting choice of doors that annihilated her recently won control.

Just one kiss, she thought, stepping boldly forward. One little bitty kiss and then nothing else—ever.

Ryan swayed instinctively back...until she grabbed a handful of shirt in each hand and pulled him closer. Raising her heels, she brushed her mouth lightly over his.

"Wha—" He abandoned the question when she released his shirt and pointed to the mistletoe over his head. He immediately grunted in remembrance, and, before Dani could step away, captured her in a bone-crushing embrace. "You know...I went to a lot of trouble to get that mistle*finger*. I think I deserve more than that poor excuse of a kiss."

"Oh *yeah?*"

"Yeah," he solemnly agreed and then crushed her lips with his.

Chapter Four

What a kiss! A shocker Ryan felt to the ends of his toes . . . and other body parts.

Dani was just as affected, judging from her wide eyes and trembling body. Her startled gaze flew to intercept his, then she backed into her bedroom and shut the door—firmly and smack in his face. Putting a hand to the tip of his nose to find out if she'd flattened it, Ryan made his way down the hall to Dani's sewing room, where Sawyer now lay on a single bed that only last night had been littered with odd-shaped cutouts of shiny white fabric and froths of netting, not to mention some other paraphernalia—probably sewing stuff—he had not recognized.

Ryan checked that Sawyer, already asleep, had enough blankets on the bed, then pulled them up under his son's chin. Sawyer smiled as though he was having sweet dreams, and love—powerful love for the boy—almost knocked Ryan off his feet. Impulsively giving in to the emotion, he bent low and brushed his lips over Sawyer's shock of brown hair.

When his son stirred, Ryan jerked back, suddenly embarrassed by the display of affection even though he shouldn't be.

Shaking his head in bemusement—this fatherhood role wasn't so simple as he'd once believed—he left the sewing room and headed to his own sleeping quarters, a delicately furnished guest room that he guessed had been Dani's during her childhood. Rose-patterned wallpaper adorned the walls, and a pale pink comforter covered the single, four-poster bed. Ruffled curtains hung from the windows and matching throw pillows decorated the window seat.

A man used to the Spartan furnishings of a bunkhouse, Ryan had to admit the room made him feel like the proverbial bull in the china shop, even as it reminded him of something his own ranch would never have—a woman's touch.

Lost in his thoughts—shockingly regretful—Ryan gathered up a pair of sweatpants and clean undershorts, and walked to the bathroom for a shower. Fifteen minutes later, he emerged, still a little damp around the gills, and went back to his bedroom. Shivering slightly in response to the chill of night now penetrating the walls of the house, Ryan slipped between crisp, pastel sheets and thumped his pillow a couple of times to get it just right. Fatigue caught up in a rush. Closing his eyes, Ryan welcomed the sleep that would save him from analyzing all that had happened to him the past two days.

Music filled Ryan's head—deafening, with a honky-tonk beat. He looked around, noting the familiar sights and sounds of a Friday night at the Spur and Saddle Bar, where he and his friends used to wind down after a week's labors. Ryan heard the melodious thump-thump of boots as a dozen or more cowboys and their ladies performed the steps of an intricate line dance on the scuffed wooden floor. He smelled beer, cigarettes and hot grease.

A familiar scene, this. One he usually loved. Tonight, however, he itched to leave, and more than once glanced longingly toward the door until finally he found himself on his feet and making his way through the crowded room to the exit that he knew opened onto the graveled parking lot.

But on stepping through it, Ryan stood not among parked cars, but on a front porch he had never seen before, but knew was his own. Baffled, pulled as if by a magnet, Ryan reached out to open the door, which swung inward before he ever touched it.

As though he were a ghost come to haunt, Ryan moved effortlessly through his foyer and down a short hallway that was familiar, but not. Tension began to simmer, then boil inside him with every step toward a door at the end of the hall. When he reached it, he found himself on the threshold of a kitchen, and he saw that someone was there...a woman...standing with her back to him.

As if on cue, she slowly turned. It was Dani, a smile of welcome on her face. Complete and utter peace washed instantly over Ryan—a tidal wave of emotion that threatened his equilibrium even while it told him he was home... home...home....

Home? Ryan woke with a start—sweating, breathless, wired. For long moments he lay in confusion, his thoughts on the disconcerting dream. His subconscious speaking? he couldn't help wondering. The next moment, he was berating himself for his foolishness. Dreams were simply the brain's way of sorting through and filing away the confusion that was life. They were a melding of fleeting thoughts, fragmented impressions, unfortunate fantasy. They were a Technicolor motion picture that, while based in things familiar, was never reality and never, ever prophecy.

So why had Dani been in his dream? Ryan wasn't sure, but guessed it had something to do with her hospitality or the fact that she turned him on. Whatever the reason she'd starred in tonight's movie-dream, there was no role for her in the life's dream he pursued by day. *That* he knew for sure.

Ryan, now wide awake and certain he'd never get back to sleep, glanced at the clock on the nightstand. It was 4:00 a.m. Not too early to get up and get with it, he decided, resolutely tossing back the quilts and rolling out of bed. He dressed for the weather and the job—thermal underwear, long-sleeved work shirt, jeans, thick socks, boots—then made his way to the kitchen. Ever mindful of his heavy footfall on the wooden floor, thunder in the quiet of the house, Ryan shut the kitchen door before setting to work locating the coffeepot.

He oriented himself to the day—Saturday, December 26—as he filled the pot with water, measured coffee grounds and turned on the burner of the stove. Though officially the weekend, it was just another workday, as far as he was concerned, especially since Dani's horses had not been tended to yesterday.

A bracing cup of black coffee later, Ryan donned his jacket and stepped outside and into a brisk winter wind. He blinked against the snow that stung his face, then set his sights on the barn, about fifty yards away, and headed toward it with determined steps.

Upon opening the door, Ryan found the spacious building illuminated by a single bulb that swayed in a gust and cast eerie shadows and would have given him the creeps except for the familiar smells and sounds that greeted him. In a flash, the barn aromas and soft whinnies of the horses in the long rows of stalls on either side of the alley took Ryan back to his last job, and he found himself homesick for it—a shocker. But then, it wasn't the job he missed, Ryan realized, it was the work. And since a glance at his watch revealed that it was now four-thirty, he took pleasure in getting started earning his and Sawyer's keep.

Ryan strode down the alley to what he guessed was the tack room. His thoughts on Wyoming and the ranch he would soon purchase with money saved his whole life, he flipped on the light switch and examined his surroundings. Ryan found them immaculate, quite a contrast to the toolshed. Clearly, this was where Dani's priorities lay, but he'd guessed that already since the huge barn was as well maintained as the main house.

Ryan stepped out a back door and next explored the fenced barnyard as best he could in the soft gray light, breaking the ice on the water in the trough so the horses could drink when they ventured from the barn. He noted that there was still plenty of hay, but the feed bin needed filling. In minutes, Ryan located the grain and heaped up the bin, then headed into the barn to look over the horses Dani had told him she boarded for some of the locals.

There were ten horses of various breeds, each in a separate stall that opened by gate to the inside of the barn and by door to the yard outside. After turning on the overhead lights, Ryan made the acquaintance of each, lingering for several minutes at the stall of a beautiful Arabian.

"His name is Ali Baby."

Ryan started at the sound of Dani's voice, then turned to find that she'd entered the barn and now stood mere feet from him. Lost in his admiration of the horses, he hadn't heard her come in. "Good morning."

"'Morning," she said. "How'd you sleep?"

"Great. Perfect," Ryan replied, perhaps a shade too heartily. He took appreciative note of his temporary employer, whose hair looked as if she'd barely run a brush through it, and whose just-waked flush he found sexy as all get out. "Yours?" he asked with a nod toward the Arabian.

"Mine," she confirmed, joining him at the stall. "Tonto is, too," she added, stepping to the next stall. The Appaloosa there whinnied a greeting, nuzzled her cheek and took the sugar cube she offered him. "You and Sawyer may ride either of them whenever you like, and there are four others that it's all right to exercise. I'll show you which ones later."

"Thanks." Ryan's gaze found and focused on her mouth, as bare of lipstick as her face was of makeup. He thought of last night's kiss and immediately wanted another. Would she go for it? he wondered. Better yet, would she consider a roll in the hay, of which there was plenty in the loft overhead?

"Come on," Dani said, words that thrilled Ryan . . . until he realized she just wanted to show him around the place.

Aiming a swift mental kick at his backside—and with the pointy toe of his boot!—Ryan followed for about three steps, then halted. "I know my way around the barn, Dani. I've already done a little exploring in here and out in the yard."

"Oh, sure. So let's go out front. I want to show you something."

Without another word, she turned on the heel of her boot and led the way to the double wooden doors, mounted to slide, through which she had so silently entered the barn moments earlier. Dani waited until Ryan caught up with her, then strode to a fence to the west of the barn, beyond which lay the snow-covered ground that was her land.

"This is the eastern border of my pasture," Dani commented, glancing at Ryan, who, in her opinion, looked ruggedly handsome this morning. Suddenly she thought of the kiss they'd shared the night before. Mmm, nice.

Nice?

Dani almost laughed aloud. If that kiss was *nice,* what would a naughty one do to her?

"My, um, cattle are accessible by horseback or truck. You'll need to break the ice on the pond, put out hay and grain and check for winter calves." As if he didn't know.

"Yes, ma'am," Ryan replied with no hint of sarcasm as far as she could tell, even though she'd just instructed him in tasks he'd probably performed for years. "How big's the pasture?"

"Two hundred acres," she replied, thankful he'd asked that instead of how big her spread was. She hated to lie, but hated even worse to tell him that she owned one thousand acres in all, eight hundred of which were leased to another rancher for pasture at the moment. "The truck's in the garage. Here's the key. She's old—a '75—and hasn't been cranked in a couple of months, but I guarantee she'll start for you."

Ryan shook his head and gave her a wry grin. "Don't count on it. I've never had much luck with the ladies."

"Yeah? Well, your luck is gonna change, cowboy," Dani murmured, leading the way to the garage, stooping to catch hold of the handle. Ryan was at her side in a flash, helping her raise the door, which creaked in protest, then peering into the shadowy interior of the one-vehicle garage.

Dani knew what he'd see—a pickup truck in surprisingly good shape considering the two hundred thousand plus miles on it. Though Ryan said nothing, she could tell he appreciated what lay before him, and she watched in amusement as he walked completely around the vehicle once, then opened the door on the driver's side and slipped behind the steering wheel.

After a moment of what appeared to be silent admiration, Ryan stuck the key in the ignition and gave it a twist. When the engine roared to life, he laughed and gave Dani a thumbs-up, but almost instantly the truck began to sputter and cough and then died.

"Probably just needs a tune-up," he commented, getting out of the truck and walking to the front. He raised the hood, then disappeared behind it. "And an oil change, not to mention a new filter. I'll check the belts, too, and take care of whatever else she needs."

Dani had to smile at his echo of her earlier *she.* "Now, don't go making promises you can't keep. You're only going to be here a few days, after all, and—"

Abruptly Ryan stuck his head out from behind the raised hood. He had the oddest look on his face—a look that stopped Dani cold.

"Would you believe that just for a minute I forgot what a short-timer I am?" He gave a brief laugh. "Don't know why. I mean, I can hardly wait to get a place of my own...." He hesitated, clearly lost in speculation. "Maybe it's the size of your ranch...smaller than any I've worked and more laid-back. Or maybe it's the way you took me and my boy in and never...not for a minute...made us feel like second-class citizens even though we were as good as on the street." Ryan shrugged. "Hell, I don't know why. I just know I'm comfortable here. I just know I like it."

"I'm glad to hear that," Dani said, struggling to keep her voice emotionless and steady. It wasn't easy. Her heart beat double time and right in her throat. Her knees were wobbly as a dish of Jell-O. Sensitivity in a cowboy? It was almost too much for the faint of heart and weak of mind.

Apparently oblivious to her symptoms, Ryan glanced at his watch then toward the house. "Five o'clock. Guess I'd better haul Sawyer out of bed."

"While you do that, I'll cook breakfast," Dani said. "Are eggs okay?"

"Eggs are fine."

Neither said another word during the walk to the house. She thought she felt his gaze on her once as they covered the distance, and risked a peek from the corner of her eye to verify it. But no. His eye was on his destination and his thoughts, no doubt, on his son and the work they had to do.

Unfortunately, Dani's thoughts weren't on her work, but on Ryan, a cowboy too good to be true, a cowboy too close for comfort. Was he all he appeared to be? she wondered. Or was he like a couple of other cowboys she'd known—a man with a private agenda and no qualms about using a woman if she could give him what he wanted?

"I scrambled the eggs," Dani said to her hired hands barely a half hour later. She set a bowlful on the table, then slipped into her chair. "I hope that's okay."

"Just the way I like 'em," Sawyer replied in a manner that warned he'd one day be as smooth-talking as his dad.

Unable to keep from responding to that boyish charm, Dani smiled and passed him the heaped-up bowl. "This food is the fuel that's going to keep you warm until lunch, you know."

"Then I'd better fill 'er up!" Sawyer exclaimed, patting his tummy before reaching for the eggs. His cheeks glowed as though from a vigorous scrubbing. His hair, slightly damp, had been neatly parted and combed back. Dressed in a wrinkled flannel shirt, jeans and boots, he looked like a miniature of his dad, and Dani wondered briefly what Ryan's childhood had been like.

She hoped it had been as happy as hers had been, at least until her beloved father died. Things had definitely begun a downhill skid at that point, culminating in what Dani considered the disaster of her mother's remarriage. Dani's stepfather, Duke Littlejohn, who just happened to be one of those men with a private agenda, had first caused her distrust of cowboys. Her ex-husband, Mick, had cinched it.

"What kind of work are we going to do, Dad?" Sawyer asked, breaking into her bitter thoughts.

Ryan listed not only what he and Dani had already discussed, but other tasks, as well.

Amazed by how quickly he'd assessed what needed to be done, Dani heard herself say, "Good eye, Ryan. I wish I could hire a ranch manager as smart as you." Only belatedly did she notice that Sawyer's expressive eyes had rounded in amazement. Guessing why, Dani reached out and touched his shoulder. "Everything won't get done today," she said to reassure him. "After all, you two will be with me at least until Monday, maybe longer."

"If we could live here forever, my dad would work for free," Sawyer commented, no doubt assuming—as Ryan probably did—that she couldn't hire his dad because she couldn't afford him.

Dani didn't set them straight. "Oh, he would, would he?" she teased, relaxed in her certainty that Ryan wouldn't be so hot on the idea.

"Sure," Sawyer said before his dad could comment. "And the three of us would be a family. You'd be the dad. I'd be the kid. He'd be—" he gave her an impish grin "—the mom!"

Dani laughed at his foolishness, but a glance at Ryan revealed he wasn't as amused. She wondered why...but not for long.

"But what about our ranch in Wyoming?" Ryan asked. "You haven't changed your mind about our finding ourselves one, have you?"

Sawyer gave his head a quick shake of denial. "I was just pretending."

"Pretending *is* fun, isn't it?" Dani murmured, remembering all the times she'd played house—or was it *ranch?*—as a youngster. Taking root in that little-girl make-believe had been the dream to be a rancher's wife. From that now-abandoned dream had stemmed her college major of home economics, as well as her marriage to a rodeo star who'd promptly talked her into turning over management of her ranch to him.

"But you have to remember that's all it is...pretending." Ryan looked really troubled now. "As soon as we get our money, we're moving on."

"I know," Sawyer replied.

What is this? Dani wondered, the next instant realizing that Ryan had just warned his son not to get too attached to people and things. Well, that warning was a good one, she thought. One she would heed, too, if she had any sense at all.

And when was I ever known for my good sense? Dani asked herself, her thoughts once again on Mick, who'd crossed her mind too many times today. This particular time, she recalled how he'd immediately set out to destroy her self-confidence with his constant criticism—an attempt to keep her ignorant of ranch matters, she now knew—and how he'd then undermined her reputation with the other ranchers in the area by reneging on promises she'd made.

Worse, he'd sold the timber rights to her land to Duke Littlejohn. It was this betrayal that finally made her realize he was more interested in what she had than in who she was.

Bothered by her thoughts, Dani swallowed a last bite of toast, then scooted back her chair and stood. "If you two will excuse me, I really need to get busy on that wedding dress. Scrape any scraps into the trash, please, and leave your plates and forks on the counter. I'll see you at lunch."

That said, she headed to the sewing room, with every step pushing the morning's pesky memories into the corner of her mind. It took only a moment to spread out her sewing things, thanks to the fact that Sawyer had made his bed.

Mere minutes after entering the sewing room, she felt as if she'd been there for hours, surrounded by yards of fabric, thread, lace, tissue patterns, netting, even a pearl-encrusted headpiece. Dani turned on the radio for company, then got to work stitching together the lace bodice, lining it, and finishing all exposed seams.

Next she put in the zipper, a task she was in the middle of when Sawyer suddenly appeared in the doorway with a paper plate in one hand and a cola in the other. When a glance at the plate revealed it laden with a sandwich and potato chips, Dani's gaze flew to the clock beside the bed—noon!

"I can't believe it's so late!" she exclaimed, taking the plate and the drink.

Sawyer just grinned and walked back out the door.

"Thanks," Dani called after him.

Suddenly realizing how hungry she was, Dani attacked the thick sandwich, intending to finish it right where she sat, at the sewing machine. Two bites later, however, an odd sort of loneliness set in and she trailed the child to the kitchen, where she found him and his father seated at the table.

"I want to hear how it's going," she said by way of explanation, even though both males seemed to take her sudden appearance in stride. Each taking a turn, they told her about their ride to the back forty of her pasture. Sawyer described the sights so awesome to an Arkansas native—deep snow and huge boulders among them. Ryan stuck to the business details, reporting how many head of cattle they were able to account for and the state of the stock pond.

If Sawyer's eyes had not sparkled with excitement, his gushing words would have been enough to demonstrate how much he'd enjoyed his morning. As for Ryan . . . she read in his expression a certain satisfaction. Whether from a job well done or from playing daddy, she couldn't really tell. He looked content—almost happy—and basking in the warmth of it, she was glad she'd sought their company.

Usually the house was quiet. She couldn't begin to imagine what it would sound like once her guests—or were they employees?—moved on. *Quiet* would become oppressive, she suspected, but that was just too bad. Opening her house to anyone on a long-term basis also meant opening her heart. And as that morning's little jaunt down memory lane had proved, Mick's betrayal still haunted her. Dani doubted that she'd ever really trust another man, even one like Ryan—a paragon among cowboys, at least so far.

The moment they finished eating, Ryan and Sawyer went back outdoors. Dani stood at the window for several minutes, watching as they started and then tinkered with the truck engine. Safe behind the curtain, she admired the fit of Ryan's jeans and let her gaze linger on what it shouldn't—his backside. There was nothing like a pair of Levi's to set off a cute butt, she decided, an errant thought that made her laugh.

At that instant, Ryan looked toward the house, waved at her, then joined his son, now sitting in the cab of the pickup. In a flash, they were rolling, no doubt to check out another section of pasture. Dani, somewhat flustered by Ryan's wave—she hadn't realized he could see her peeking out at him—watched Sawyer jump from the truck to open and close the fence as the vehicle passed through it. Moments later, they disappeared into a stand of evergreens, the old truck bobbing and lurching over the frozen, snow-covered ruts of the trail.

Dani left the window and walked to the sink, into which she began to run hot water. After squirting a generous amount of dishwashing liquid into it, she transferred the breakfast and lunch dishes to the suds, where she left them to soak.

How nice it would be, she thought, to have no more to worry about than a few dirty dishes and what to cook for the next meal. How nice to let a man she trusted take care of the complicated business of ranching, while she took care of him.

An old-fashioned desire? Well, if not that, then a very traditional one she had outgrown. Nonetheless, Dani stole a moment to follow Sawyer's lead, *pretending* that Ryan was her husband, and his son, theirs. The old dream felt shockingly, frighteningly good—enough to make her shake her head and marvel that she could be so out of step with the rest of the world. Hadn't her bad marriage taught her anything?

Apparently not, Dani realized with a heavy sigh. Determined to throw off her weird mood, she walked back to the sewing room and concentrated on the task at hand—piecing together the most beautiful gown in the world. The irony of her situation did not escape her, of course—a woman who no longer believed in weddings creating a dress to be worn in one.

For two hours she worked without stopping, in that time finishing the bodice and attaching it with pins to the skirt, which didn't want to hang right. After a short break to stretch her legs, Dani impulsively slipped out of her clothes and into the dress to assess the problem. After all, she was pretty much the same body build as the bride. If the skirt didn't look better when Barbara tried it on, some sort of adjustment would have to be made until it did.

Carefully, Dani zipped the dress. She moved toward the door, intending to walk down the hall to her bedroom and the full-length mirror mounted on the back of the door. But before she made it out of the room, Sawyer burst into it.

"We found a calf!" the boy exclaimed, so excited he fairly danced around her. The next instant, his jaw dropped and he froze to the spot. "Wow!"

"Does that mean you like it?" Dani asked, bubbling with laughter at his awestruck expression. She pirouetted slowly, stopping when she faced him again, her back to the door.

"Yes, ma'am!" Sawyer replied.

"And that goes double for me."

Dani whirled at the sound of Ryan's voice and found him standing in the doorway. His gaze taking in every millimeter of her from top to toe, he walked slowly into the room.

"My God," he murmured. "You look so... different."

"Yeah," Sawyer agreed. "You look real good." The next instant he winced when his dad elbowed him.

"Sawyer doesn't mean that you didn't look good before," Ryan quickly explained.

Dani just smiled. Dressed as she usually was in work shirt and jeans, how could she ever really look "good"? "If you guys will excuse me...?" She took one step toward the door, then turned back to Sawyer. "Where's the calf, by the way?"

"In the barn. His mama is, too. She followed us in just like Dad said she would."

"Good," Dani commented, leaving them and moving down the hall to her bedroom. She heard Ryan say something to Sawyer, then the soft clump of boots as they headed in the opposite direction.

A second later found her examining the dress in the mirror, realizing what the problem was and placing a strategic pin where a nip and tuck was required. Her thoughts were not on the adjustment, but on her guests, who undoubtedly saw her as a plain Jane. The idea bothered Dani immensely and so distracted her that she stuck herself with one of the pins.

Grabbing one of the tissues in a box on her dresser, Dani pressed it to the blood oozing out of the tiny wound. All she needed was a bright red spot on this snow-white garment.

"Are you okay?"

Dani jumped at the question and glanced in disbelief at the mirror before her. Reflected in it, she saw Ryan, who had not gone outside, but had followed her to the bedroom.

"It's just a tiny stick," Dani snapped, vastly irritated with him. How could a man wearing boots slip up on anyone?

"I'm not talking about that."

Realizing that he must be referring to her bad mood, Dani slipped past him without a word and hurried to the sewing room. When he attempted to follow her inside, she pushed him back out and shut the door with a brisk, "I have to get out of this dress before I bleed on it."

Doing that wasn't so easy, however, since she had to accomplish the feat left-handed. To make matters worse, the zipper slide stuck midway down, an impossible spot to reach.

With a soft "Dammit!," Dani stalked to the door and threw it open wide so she could motion Ryan inside. He joined her in a flash and, when she presented her back to him, began to pull on the slide.

"Be careful," Dani grumbled. "This fabric is very delicate."

"I am being careful," Ryan told her even as he yanked. Suddenly, the slide was free and, in one smooth move, lowered all the way down.

Dani instantly spun around so he couldn't get an eyeful of her mauve panties and bra, which were anything but plain

Jane. With a mumbled thanks, she began to shoo him toward the door again.

"Not until you tell me why you're upset," Ryan said, halting their progress easily.

"I'm not upset," Dani lied, in the next breath somewhat tartly adding, "Dresses really have no place on a ranch, you know."

"I never said they did." Ryan, looking totally baffled by her comment, abruptly let her usher him into the hall.

Dani quickly changed into her own clothes, hung up the dress, waited five extra minutes, then opened the door and peeked out to see if he'd given up and gone.

He hadn't. "Lady, you've got one hell of a chip on your shoulder, you know it?"

"I do not."

"Sure you do... if you let the words of an eight-year-old kid get you down. He didn't mean that the way it sounded. Why, just yesterday...when we were making that card...he saw that picture of you on your office wall and commented that you were the most beautiful lady in Colorado."

Dani, who now stood in the middle of the sewing room with Ryan not two feet away, struggled not to laugh. "And what did you say?"

"I agreed, of course."

Dani gave in to her mirth at that—a display of humor that clearly irritated Ryan.

"You think I'm lying."

"Yes, though now that I think about it, you may not be. I mean, you've only been in the state a couple of days and were in the trunk of my car some of that time." Shaking her head, she started to step toward the sewing machine, but found herself caught by the shoulders and held in place.

For long moments, Ryan said nothing, his stare so intense that Dani actually began to squirm. Then he let her go. "Who did this to you, Dani?"

"Did what?" she asked, though she suspected she knew to what he referred.

"Shattered your self-esteem. Who did it? That ex of yours?"

Dani hesitated before her heavy sigh and confession. "He did his part, I guess, and so did my mother, who was forever nagging me about my clothes, my hair, my weight." She sighed. "It's easier to believe the bad stuff than the good."

"Yeah," Ryan murmured as if he knew exactly what she was talking about, as if his self-esteem had been annihilated once, too. "Especially when the bad stuff comes from someone you love and trust."

With another sigh and a nod, Dani sat on the edge of Sawyer's bed. Ryan joined her there a moment later and sat in silence about a foot away, his gaze on the floor.

"I'm sorry I overreacted." She gave him a rueful smile.

"No sweat," he replied, smiling back.

"Do you think Sawyer could tell I was upset?"

"I doubt it. He had his mind on that calf, which is the reason he made the comment in the first place. He wasn't paying attention."

Dani laughed, all at once feeling better and past ready to change the subject. "The calf's going to be okay?"

"The calf will be fine. I told Sawyer you'd be out in a bit to check on it."

"Okay." Dani sprang to her feet, fully intending to go to the barn. To her surprise, Ryan caught her hand in his and halted her escape.

"Before we go, I have something I want to say, something you can believe." Ryan stood. "You're a natural beauty, Dani,'' he said, brushing his fingers over her flushed cheek, then playfully tugging a lock of her hair. ''In fact, I think I'd be safe in saying you're one of those women all other women must hate, the kind who looks great in anything, the kind who'd look best in nothing.''

Chapter Five

Though Ryan knew he deserved to have his face slapped for his hopeful comment, Dani just laughed at him. He traced her smile with his finger, felt her suddenly shiver.

"Cold?" he asked in disbelief. He, himself, was hot. *Very* hot. Nonetheless, he began to rub her shoulders and her upper arms vigorously to chase away any chill.

"I am *not* cold," she told him, halting his efforts. For a millisecond, they stood just that way—face-to-face, her hands holding his. Then she suddenly let go of him, framed his face with her palms and stepped close enough to brush her lips over his.

Stunned, Ryan did what came naturally and wrapped his arms around her. He pulled Dani close—and closer—until their lips met again in a crushing kiss, all the while moving his hands over her back somewhat tentatively since he didn't want to scare her off. Mimicking Ryan, Dani moved her hands over him, too, then tucked them in his rear pockets, an action that pulled his lower body closer.

Hot damsel...hot damn! Boldly, Ryan slid his hands lower and firmly molded the curve of her hips. When she wiggled, not in protest, but to get closer still, he grunted his approval, tightened the embrace, and, lifting her right off her feet, stepped backward the two steps to the bed.

He sat, then fell back on the bed, taking her with him. Being attached as they were made the move an awkward one, and as she settled on top of him, he felt one of her knees brush his privates, a near miss that made his life flash before his eyes.

"Oops, sorry," she murmured, crimson-faced and instantly trying to scramble off.

Ryan did not allow it. Instead, he spread his legs enough that she rode one thigh with her knees pressed into the mattress instead of him. Holding her just there, he began to plant kisses on her chin, cheeks and mouth.

At first, Dani seemed a little uncertain about this new arrangement. Red light? he naturally wondered. Before he could find out or release her, she relaxed and gave him her full weight. Ryan relished the way her breasts crushed to his chest, loved the fact that every breath she took was now his.

They kissed again—a gentle mating of lips. This tender testing and tasting set Ryan on fire. Holding her tightly, he abruptly turned on his side, a change in position that put her on the bed next to him. Legs still tangled, hearts thumping wildly, they kissed and touched. Ryan bravely led the way, taking every liberty Dani would allow.

He trailed his fingers over her neck. He cupped her breasts through the flannel of her shirt. He began to unbutton that faded winter garment...always waiting for the "Stop!" that would end this heaven on earth.

It never came. Instead, she did some unbuttoning of her own, huffing her impatience when she uncovered, not his bare chest, but a worn thermal undershirt.

Ryan chuckled. She smiled. They kissed again—a kiss that was unbelievably hotter, wetter, longer.

Suddenly, a door slammed somewhere in the house.

"Dad! Dani!"

With a heartfelt curse, Ryan fell back on the bed and struggled to free his legs. Dani was quicker, somehow slipping loose and leaping up beside the bed, where she stood, her back to the entrance of the room while she hurriedly buttoned her blouse.

Ryan looked toward the door and found Sawyer standing there, face solemn, eyes narrowed. Just how much had the boy seen?

"Are you guys coming or what?"

Dani blanched at the innocent question. With a wide-eyed glance over her shoulder at Ryan, she spun on her heel, quickly slipped past his son and vanished down the hall.

As rattled as she was by Sawyer's unfortunate choice of words, Ryan awkwardly finger-combed his hair, smoothed his half-buttoned shirt and stood.

"We're, um, coming. But first, I'd better explain what we were doing." He joined his son at the door.

Sawyer shook his head and grimaced. "I already know."

"You do?" Surely this eight-year-old boy hadn't heard about the birds and the bees.

Sawyer nodded.

"I see. Well, is there anything you want to ask me?"

Again, Sawyer nodded.

Ryan waited, dreading the question, yet knowing he deserved whatever grief his young son gave him.

"Is Dani going to have a baby now?"

"Holy—" Catching himself, Ryan sucked in a calming breath and managed a shaky smile. "A man and a woman have to get really, really close to make a baby, son. Much closer than Dani and I were."

"Oh."

"Would you, er, like for me to explain how it works?"

Sawyer considered his dad's offer for what seemed an eternity, then shook his head. "Uh-uh. I'd rather go look at the calf."

"Okay. Sure." Whew!

"You can tell me tonight."

Ryan gulped and accepted his fate with grace and a decided lack of enthusiasm. "Tonight... right." Absently patting his son's hair—man oh man, were kids a pickup load of responsibility!—he directed them out of the sewing room and down the hall to the kitchen, where Dani stood, sipping ice water. Ryan reached for her glass, and, when she dutifully handed it to him, drank half the contents in one swallow, all the while wishing he could shower in it.

"Ready to go look at your calf?" she asked Sawyer a little too brightly.

"Mine? *She's mine?*" Sawyer's eyes grew round as a Christmas ornament.

"If you want him... and your dad says it's okay." Obviously realizing she should've consulted Ryan *before* she gave the gift, Dani shot him a questioning glance.

Charity? Ryan wondered, but only for a second. Somehow, he knew it wasn't that, but a gift from the heart. She was the kind of woman who gave like that—a woman who was warm, loving, generous to a fault.

He frowned slightly. Was that what their near sex had been? A gift from the heart? Lord, but he hoped not. Ryan wanted no such gift from her, from any woman. Such a gift put a man on the spot, making it hard—if not impossible—to reject what she gave, even though he knew it could change his plans and complicate his life beyond measure.

"Dad?" Sawyer waited for his answer.

"It's okay with me," Ryan said, suddenly coming to life, "But the calf is your responsibility."

"Yes, sir!" Sawyer exclaimed, dashing out the door. Ryan heard a loud "Whoopee!" outside and laughed, as did Dani.

Their eyes met. She had the grace to blush. "Sorry I skedaddled a minute ago, but I'm not that good with kids, I didn't have a clue what to say to him."

"And you thought I would?"

Dani shrugged. "You're his dad."

"Yeah, well, *this kid* did not come with directions, lady, and I'm sure as hell no natural-born expert." He shook his head, thinking about what had been said and what still needed to be...both to his son and, if he was smart, to Dani. But how did a man go about telling a woman that while he'd willingly accept the gift of her body, he'd rather her heart were not in it? "Sawyer and I are going to talk about the birds and bees tonight. Care to join us?"

Dani grimaced. "I think I'll pass."

"But this is half your fault."

"And all your problem." That said, she spun toward the door, only to stop when Ryan seized the moment—*and* a handful of her shirt. Throwing caution to the wind, he tugged firmly on it and drew her back to him, which she resisted only slightly. Ryan turned Dani around, then dipped his head and kissed her... hard... on the lips.

"Guess again, Dani," he said before scooping his hat up off the kitchen counter. Settling it on his head, he touched the brim in a brief salute, then followed his son outdoors.

Sawyer's excitement was as contagious as the measles, but a lot more fun. Out in the barn, watching him with the gangly calf, Dani once again strolled back in time to the good ol' days of her childhood. Her dad had given her a calf just like this one and she recalled being every bit as thrilled as Sawyer.

"You know," Ryan commented from where he knelt on one knee in the hay by the calf. "I believe I was eight when I got my first calf. No, I was just seven, now that I think about it. Eight was when my parents divorced."

So he came from a broken home. Dani wondered briefly how that had impacted on him. Was he a worse father for it—lacking a role model? Or was he a better one? A parent who tried extra hard to do the right thing?

"Must be a ranching tradition," Dani said, adding, "The calf, I mean, not the divorce. Did your mother remarry?"

"Yes, when I was ten." Ryan got to his feet.

"Did your new dad give you a calf, too?" Sawyer didn't stand, but sprawled in the hay as though intending to spend the rest of the day in the barn, watching his new pet.

"All I got from him was a hard time," Ryan muttered with obvious bitterness. "Which is why I left home when I was sixteen. Went to work on a ranch just a little bigger than this one."

"Did you like it?" asked Sawyer, clearly enthralled by the tale.

"I did."

Though Dani wished Sawyer would ask more questions—there was so much she wanted to know—in typical child fashion, he lost interest and changed the subject. "What should I name her, Dad?"

"Think on it a day or two. I'm sure you'll come up with something."

"Okay," Sawyer good-naturedly agreed.

Dani left them to their work shortly after, slowly walking back to the house through gently falling snow. She paused in the kitchen to finish her water and instantly recalled the way Ryan had taken it from her. Just the memory of how he'd looked at that moment—so virile, so wired, so *frustrated*—made her body heat up a degree or two. She dared not recall what it felt like to be touched, much less kissed, by him.

Just how far would they have gone had Sawyer not appeared? she had to wonder. In a flash she knew the answer—too far. Not one to sleep around, Dani wondered what it was about this man that compromised her morals, obliterated her resolve. For over a year, she'd avoided romantic entanglements, tactfully but firmly refusing the advances of every hopeful cowboy who'd met her at one place or another and then called or dropped by. There'd been several. She'd remained free.

Then along came Ryan. And how had she greeted the man? With a *come on in!* of all things. And him a man just passing through.

Just passing through?

The words echoed loudly in Dani's head, and, suddenly, she had her answer. He *was* just passing through—in theory, no real threat to her at all. He did not want her heart. He did not want her ranch. All he wanted was her body. And all she wanted was his.

So simple. So dangerous.

Fool!

Dani pushed herself to complete the wedding dress that day, stopping only long enough midafternoon to make a pot of chili for Ryan and Sawyer to eat when they finally came indoors.

She skipped supper, herself, though she did take a short break while they were eating so she could hear what they'd accomplished. It turned out to be a lot more than she'd expected, and once again she wished for a ranch manager to take up the worry of keeping the place going. It wasn't as if she couldn't afford the salary. Thanks to her cattle, her rental income and her guest horses, she could.

No, it was a matter of trust. A fear of turning over too much control, of being cheated again, of losing all she owned and loved.

Since the guys volunteered to wash dishes, Dani soon found herself at her sewing machine again. Thanks to the fact that Ryan had tucked Sawyer into her bed and thus freed up the sewing room, she stayed there until the living-room clock loudly announced midnight. As the clock slowly chimed the hour, she knotted her thread for the last time, securing a final pearl to the bodice of what was now a beautiful wedding gown.

Barbara would be a bride to remember, Dani thought, and was surprised by a sharp stab of what could only be jealousy. *Am I really so envious of Barb?* she asked herself.

Shaking her head in bemusement, Dani put the dress on a satin-covered hanger, slipped a clear plastic bag over it and closed shop. Tomorrow would be soon enough to clean up beyond clearing off the bed. Now she wanted a hot shower and cool sheets.

Dani doused the light and made her way quietly down the pitch-black hall, unwilling to wake her guests. As she reached the bathroom door, she detected a blur of movement, and, before she could put on her brakes, crashed into Ryan, just stepping into the hall.

In a flash, he wrapped his arms around her middle and backed into the bathroom, shutting the door with his bare foot. He then fumbled in the dark for the lock, which finally clicked ominously into place, for the moment securing them from the rest of the world.

Uh-oh, Dani thought even as her heart began to thump in anticipation.

"All I want is a shower." Her voice, her body, quivered with the lie. Could he hear it, feel it?

"First you have to make amends for running out on me today."

"You managed okay."

"Oh yeah, sure. I did a great job convincing my son you weren't going to have my baby."

Dani gasped. "Is that what he thought?"

"That's exactly what he thought... but I set him straight tonight." Ryan winced at the memory, an expression Dani saw clearly in the half-light left over from the security bulb mounted on a pole outside.

"Oh, God, I'm sorry."

"And you admit that you owe me?"

Gulp. "Depends on my penance, I guess."

"How about this?" he asked, pinning her to the door with his body, nuzzling her neck.

Dani tipped her head slightly to give him better access. "I—I could go for that."

"What... about... this?" He trailed his mouth to her earlobe, to her cheek, to her mouth.

"Mmm," was all Dani could reply, an answer he apparently took for the whopping *yes!* it was. With effort, she turned her face to the side and caught her breath.

"Relax," Ryan softly urged as he traced a path with his fingers up her arms, over her shoulders and down to her breasts.

Relax? He had to be kidding. Dani couldn't remember when last she'd been so sexually stimulated. The man drove her wild. There was no denying it.

Giving in to need, she slipped her arms around his neck and locked her hands behind his head. With a firm tug, she pulled his face closer and pressed her lips to his. They kissed, not once, but over and over and over.

"Sawyer...?" she somehow managed to whisper, voicing a concern that could not be ignored.

"Doesn't have to know." The words fanned her face.

"But if he wakes up?"

"He sleeps like a log, Dani. He won't wake up."

With a sigh, Dani let go of that objection to this glorious closeness. Others quickly crowded her mind, begging for notice. She ignored them, promising later...later....

His touch firm and sure, Ryan unbuttoned enough buttons to Dani's shirt so that he could pull it off over her head. Obediently, she raised her arms, allowing him that freedom. He paused, a look of utter reverence on his face, before unclasping the front closure of her lacy bra. As the garment fell open, he touched her, at first tentatively, then with the intention she'd come to know. Unwilling to experience but not participate, Dani skimmed her fingertips over his bare back, laughing softly when his muscles jumped in response.

Heaven was standing so close to a man again. Hell was how sorry she'd be when he left her. And he would leave her. A night of passion would not change a thing.

Or would it? Unbidden, memories of another seduction flooded Dani. Oh, they hadn't been in the bathroom—she and Mick—but they'd stood this close in the dark of night and loved each other in just this way.

Loved each other? She nearly laughed aloud at that falsehood. Only one of them had been in love: Dani. Mick's actions that night were nothing more than a carefully thought-out strategy to win her love and her trust.

Was this encounter the same? she wondered. Had Ryan changed his mind about Wyoming? Was he now a man with a plan, and a foolish, lonely ranch owner in his sights?

As if sensing the withdrawal that naturally accompanied her negative thoughts, Ryan shifted his attention from her thoroughly suckled breasts to her face. For just a second he studied her expression, during which Dani struggled not to reveal what she was thinking.

"Let's take a shower." He spoke the words as if he didn't believe she'd agree to the idea, as if he was testing to see how far-gone she really was.

Dani swallowed hard. What to answer...? What to say...? Safest would be *no.* But if his motives were really pure, after all, then she'd have thrown away the physical comfort of a very special cowboy, something a woman such as she could not afford to do.

"Ryan, I—" Dani hushed. Was that the telephone?

"What...?"

"Do you hear the telephone?"

"At one o'clock in the morning? Stop looking for a way out, Dani." He tucked his fingers under her chin and tipped her head back, raising her gaze to his.

In the heavy silence that followed, Dani again heard what could only be the telephone—muffled to them, locked away as they were in the bathroom, but undoubtedly loud to the rest of the house. Ryan tensed at once, proof he heard the sound, too.

"Well, hell." He stepped back as though freeing *her* to make a dash to answer it.

Dani just crossed her arms over her bare breasts and frantically motioned him to do the honors, which he did at once. She heard a loud click as the lock was undone, then the ringing of the phone as he threw open the door. Ryan dashed into the hall toward the kitchen, cursing like a sailor when he caught his toe on the leg of a kitchen chair, something Dani had done a hundred times, herself. She winced, knowing how badly that hurt.

"Hello!" He as good as growled the greeting and so loudly that his son must, indeed, sleep like a log not to hear it.

Quickly, one ear tuned to the rumble of his voice, now lowered so that she could not make out words, Dani refastened her bra and snatched her shirt from the floor. Buttoning it from neck to hem, she walked to the kitchen, where Ryan stood in the dark.

"So the truck's okay?" she heard him say.

Dani's heart jumped, then sank all the way to her bare toes. They'd found his truck. He'd be leaving now.

No surprise, that. She'd known all along he would go. So why the sudden dejection? Why the threatening tears? If she wanted sex so desperately, she could easily find another cowboy to be her stud. And if she just wanted a ranch hand, there were plenty of those, too.

Suddenly Ryan laughed. "I guess the ATM card wasn't much use without the PIN, huh? Well, I know what to do with it, let me tell you." He listened for a moment, only belatedly noticing that Dani had joined him in the kitchen and now stood listening to every word. Ryan gave her a thumbs-up, just as he had from the truck that afternoon. It felt like an eternity ago.

Dani smiled at him somewhat absently, her thoughts on the time they'd spent together. It seemed months instead of days. It was almost as if each second were really an hour, giving every conversation, every encounter incredible significance.

"I don't believe it! Were there checks missing?" He winced. "God, I hope they didn't wipe out the account." Again he listened. "Right. I'll see you then. Thanks a million, Cliff."

The moment Ryan hung up, he turned to Dani. "They caught the escaped convicts in Denver. They were still traveling in my truck, which appears to be in good shape. The police didn't find any money behind the seat, so I guess I can kiss that goodbye, but they did retrieve all my things, including my checkbook, minus four checks, according to the register.'' He shook his head, clearly worried. ''I had all my money in my checking account. Of course, the balance on the register didn't reflect it, since I just made the transfer from savings to checking on Wednesday.'' He gave her a rueful grin. ''Maybe it's a good thing I'm not much of a bookkeeper.''

''As if convicts would take pains not to overdraw your account,'' Dani murmured, instantly regretting her candid comment when Ryan's grin vanished. ''But don't worry. Everything slows down during the holidays, at least bankwise. When you call first thing Monday to stop payment on those missing checks, you'll find that none of them have cleared yet.''

''You think?'' He looked very doubtful of such good fortune, and Dani's heart went out to him.

''I really do.'' She hesitated, feeling awkward and unsure of herself. Their earlier mood of passion had been shattered by the phone call. Was he in any mood to try to rebuild it?

One look at his slumped shoulders and crestfallen expression told her he was not.

Good, Dani told herself even as her body cried, *''Foul!''* ''Go to bed, Ryan. Get some sleep. Everything will look brighter tomorrow.''

''Yeah.'' He turned and started toward the door, only to halt and glance back at her as if just remembering where they'd been and what they'd been doing when the phone rang. ''Dani, I—''

''Sleep tight, Ryan.'' Somehow, she mustered a smile.

"Er, right. You, too." With a nod, he was gone, leaving Dani alone in the kitchen, which suddenly felt cold. The dark pressed in on her and, instantly gloomy, she headed to the living room instead of her bed.

Dani sat on the couch in the shadowy room, her gaze on the Christmas tree and the ornaments that somehow caught and reflected what little light there was. She curled her feet under her to hold off the wintry chill. Funny, she hadn't noticed that chill before. But then, Ryan was hot as a radiator, warming her from head to toe every time he came around.

She laid her head back and closed her eyes, letting her body unwind at will. Slowly, the tension of unsatisfied desire drained away and she began to feel somewhat better, if a little disappointed. It won't happen now, she thought. Ryan would be distracted the rest of the time he was at the ranch, his attention focused on getting his things back and moving on. Sex would be the last thing on his mind. She gave the dark a half smile. Well, maybe not the *last* thing—he was a man, after all—but sex would be low on his list of must do's, she would bet, which meant she could erase it from hers altogether.

Damn the luck.

Damn the luck? Dani's jaw dropped when she registered her own thought. Two days ago, she'd have denied to the death that she'd ever have sex with a cowboy again. Tonight, she sat alone in the dark and cursed the bad luck that had interrupted what would surely have been the hottest encounter of her life. What on earth had happened to alter her thinking so thoroughly?

What? Try *who,* her common sense replied. A who had happened—Ryan Given. Cowboy extraordinaire. Father-in-training. Mystery man. And just the thought of him sent shivers of delight dancing up her spine. He made her crazy, he did. A physical reaction she could not begin to explain since she'd never have believed anything so intense, so all-consuming could be possible.

But was it all physical? Or was her psyche involved, as well?

Could it be...could it just be that she'd fallen for him, another cowboy? And with her whole heart and soul?

Dani realized the possibility wasn't so farfetched. Heaven knew, Ryan wasn't just any old cowboy. Though ignorant of her wealth, he wanted her. And wanting her, he remained true to his dream of moving to Wyoming. She actually took comfort in knowing his plans did not hinge on her or her ranch. Never mind that she hadn't been totally honest with Ryan about the size of her spread. Even if he knew the truth, which he obviously did not, it wouldn't change a thing.

Or would it?

Chapter Six

On Sunday, December 27, Ryan and Sawyer began their day in the barn, seeing after the horses and the boy's calf. As soon as they finished up there, they walked back to the house and ate the breakfast Dani put on the table—French toast with warmed maple syrup to drizzle over it, and bacon, fried up crisp.

Ryan thought Dani seemed very distracted, saying little and avoiding his gaze. Only to Sawyer did she respond with her usual warmth. Ryan wondered if last night's near miss was to blame for her sudden coolness toward him. He wouldn't fault her for having regrets. They'd come close—too close—to showering together, which would certainly have led to the sexual encounter he'd fantasized about since he'd stumbled onto her chopping down the Christmas tree.

But was she sorry they'd put themselves in a position to almost have sex, or sorry they hadn't managed to actually have it?

Ryan, himself, regretted the former most. Dani was too good a woman to be used for sex, and using her was all he'd be doing if he slept with her and then moved on.

Still . . . she had some responsibility, some choice in this, he thought. Especially since he'd made it so plain that he intended to leave first chance he got.

"Where are you guys working this morning?" Dani asked, breaking what had become an awkward silence.

"South end of the pasture," Ryan replied. "I'm thinking we may find another calf today. If not today, then tomorrow. Mama looked almost ready."

"Another calf?" Sawyer's eyes lit up.

"Only one to a customer, sport," Ryan said, grinning when Sawyer guiltily ducked his head.

"I wasn't going to ask for it."

"Of course he wasn't," Dani quickly agreed as if she feared Ryan was going to fuss at his son. She refilled the boy's glass with milk, then set the carton on the table. "Did you ever name your calf?"

Sawyer nodded. "I'm calling her Miss Dani."

Ryan nearly choked. "You're naming the calf after Dani?"

"Uh-huh."

"But—" Ryan halted when Dani, always the peacemaker, shook her head ever so slightly at him.

"I'm very flattered," she said, adding, "But you don't have to do that, you know."

"I know," Sawyer said in the matter-of-fact way of a child. "I just don't want to forget you when we're in Wyoming. I mean, I don't have a picture or anything."

Ryan's heart twisted in his chest. Suddenly, he realized what leaving Dani would mean to Sawyer, who had nothing more than photos to remind him of the mother figures he'd loved and lost in his brief life.

"I have an idea," Ryan blurted out. "When I get my stuff back, we'll take some pictures of Dani and the ranch. A whole roll, if you like. Assuming my camera is there, that is."

"Okay," said Sawyer, "but I'm still naming the calf after her."

"Right," Ryan agreed, with a sorry-about-that shrug at their hostess. For the first time that morning, she looked him square in the eye. To his astonishment, she blushed as if she was embarrassed about something. Ryan suddenly wondered if that was what stood between them today, not regret.

Was she remembering how incredibly responsive she'd been last night? Was she wishing he'd forget?

Fat chance, he thought, shifting position to ease the sudden bind of his jeans. Dani was one luscious lady. Just thinking about her made him wish he could banish his son to the barn for a couple of hours so the two of them could take up where they'd left off.

"May I be excused?"

Ryan started at the question, then gave himself a mental shake. Some fine dad he made, slipping in and out of the role when it suited him. "After you scrape your plate and set it in the sink."

With a nod, Sawyer did as requested, then walked to the door. "Can we ride horses today instead of taking the truck?"

Ryan glanced at Dani, seeking permission. She gave it with a nod. He grinned at his son. "Think you can handle Tonto?"

"You bet!" Sawyer exclaimed as he dashed out the door and to the barn.

Ryan looked back at Dani, who got to her feet and stepped to the trash can to scrape her own plate. "What are you going to do this morning?" he asked her.

"Clean up the sewing room, for starters." She gave him a smile that did not reach her eyes, then walked to the sink. Ryan rose from the table and joined her there.

"About last night—"

"Oh, please, Ryan," she murmured, turning to face him. "Let's don't analyze it."

"Who's analyzing it?" he asked. What the hell was her problem? "I was just going to say I think you're the sexiest woman I've ever known."

Her jaw dropped.

"And I wanted to apologize," Ryan continued somewhat sheepishly. "I started that last night. I should've finished it."

"Apology accepted," Dani said, not exactly a reply that revealed what she was thinking.

"But never, ever start anything again...?" Ryan softly prompted, trying to get her to open up.

"Well, it is *my* turn."

He went totally still, wondering if she could possibly mean what he wanted her to mean. Surely the gods weren't *that* generous.

Thankfully, Dani didn't leave him curious long, but stepped close, slipped her arms around his waist and rested her cheek on his chest. Embarrassed...? Not by a long shot.

"If I seem a little distant," she murmured into his shirtfront, "it's only because I know you're going to leave, and I think I'm going to be sorry."

Her honesty was as potent as a kick to the back of the knees, leaving him decidedly off balance.

"Part of me wants to do the safe thing and push you away," she continued. "I mean, there's obviously no future for us...not that I want there to be. I really don't." She drew in a deep breath, then exhaled on a sigh. "All the same, another part of me wants to get closer, taking whatever you're willing to give. In a way, I'm just like Sawyer, I guess, wanting a memory for when you're gone." She suddenly stepped away from him and shook her head in obvious bemusement. "To say the least, I'm confused, and I'm wondering if you are, too."

Never one to verbalize his thoughts and emotions, Ryan winced at the probing question. "I just know I want you, Dani. Not for always," he hastily added, lest she consider this some kind of long-term game plan, or, God forbid, a proposal. "But for now. I realize that isn't much. Hell, that isn't anything, is it? I mean, women usually prefer an arrangement more definite, and you know I can't offer that."

"Can't or won't?"

"Does it matter?"

"Not really. The end result is the same, and the end result suits me just fine."

"Are you sure?" Somehow, he couldn't believe it.

"Oh, yes. I've been there, done that. I hated it, Ryan, hated it."

So she really and truly understood the situation and still wanted him. Ryan wished again that he could shuck the role of parent long enough to bed this willing woman before she changed her mind. "Uh, Dani?"

"Yes?"

"How do you feel about finishing this discussion at midnight tonight in your bathroom with the door locked?"

Dani tipped her head back and considered the question for several long moments. "That's not particularly romantic."

"Maybe not, but it's as private as we can get in this house." He waited several seconds longer, during which she said nothing, then huffed his impatience. "So speak to me, woman. Are we on or not?"

Clearly, Dani battled her common sense. Ryan tensed, predicting it would win. Her sudden sigh seemed to confirm the victory. Curling her finger, she motioned him to lean closer for the verdict, then put her lips to his ear.

"Last one there's a rotten egg, cowboy!" she whispered and might've said more...if his kiss hadn't gotten in the way.

Promptly at noon, Dani put the last sandwich into her backpack and zipped it closed. She smiled, not for the first time remembering the joy on Ryan's face that morning when she'd promised to meet him at midnight. It surely mirrored her own, the reason she refused to think further about what she'd done.

As for her telling him it was *her* turn to call the shots, she'd meant that and for one good reason: Dani thought that if she set the pace, she'd be better able to maintain some control over this explosive—potentially heartbreaking—situation. Nothing could happen before she meant it to, before she was mentally ready.

Dani strapped a large thermos to the outside of the pack, then slipped her arms through the loops and messed with it until it felt comfortable on her back. After scanning the counter and table for anything she might not have thought of, she tucked a waterproof sleeping bag under her arm and headed outside to the barn.

A short time later found her astride a palomino she'd nicknamed Sunshine since the registered name was too hard to remember. Woman and horse traveled as one over the rocky terrain that was her pasture, Dani taking pleasure in the sights and smells of a Colorado December.

Though it wasn't snowing yet today, the sun hid behind gray clouds that promised more of the fluffy stuff. Dani didn't really mind the threat. Picnics in the snow were fun, no matter what, and this one would be extra special since it would be Sawyer's—and probably Ryan's—first. At least she assumed it would be. Now that she thought about it, she wasn't sure how much snow Arkansas got. Oklahoma, either, for that matter. Maybe they had winter picnics all the time.

Wishing Ryan had been a little more specific about where in the south pasture he and Sawyer would be today, Dani scanned the trail ahead. She wasn't really worried, of course. She knew this area as well as she knew the barnyard. She'd find her guests. Then they'd have a wonderful time—maybe their last together since tomorrow was Monday and it would certainly be the beginning of the end of their stay with her.

As if on cue, Dani heard the echo of laughter somewhere beyond the grove of trees ahead. She reined in Sunshine and sat very still, listening. Sure enough, she heard the sound again, farther to the south. She headed in that direction at a trot. Just beyond a grove of evergreens, Dani and the palomino burst into a clearing and found Sawyer and Ryan, dismounted and on their knees in the snow as if examining something.

Curious, she approached them. When Sunshine whinnied to her barn mates, announcing their arrival from several yards away, both Ryan and Sawyer turned to look. Sawyer leaped to his feet, waving. Ryan just looked at her, no hint of welcome on his face or in his eyes.

Second thoughts? Dani wondered. She almost wished that were true. There could be no better way to avoid making what might be the biggest mistake of her life. Heaven knew, she hadn't the good sense, or will, to back out, herself.

"What are you doing?" Sawyer asked, running over to her. His sudden approach startled Sunshine, who jumped and threatened to bolt. In a flash, Ryan was there, grabbing the reins, soothing the horse with expert calm. Though Sunshine quickly settled down, Ryan reached up and caught Dani by the arm, insisting without words that she dismount *now*.

Noting Sawyer's chagrin, she did, then slipped off the backpack and held it up for all to see. "Lunch."

The boy's immediate grin stretched from ear to ear. "We're going to eat out here?"

"That's right," she told him. "A picnic in the snow. Ever had one?"

"No way!" Sawyer exclaimed. He turned to his parent. "Have you, Dad?"

Ryan shook his head. "Can't say that I have."

"Well, you guys don't know what you've been missing." She turned to Ryan. "Would you get that sleeping bag, please?" When he nodded, Dani handed the reins to Sawyer, then led the way to a patch of flat, snow-blanketed ground not far from a towering Limber pine. "Here looks like the perfect spot," she announced, belatedly noticing animal tracks in the snow. So that's what they'd been looking at.

"I see we've had a trespasser," she commented, pointing to the tracks.

"A deer," Sawyer informed her confidently as he looped Sunshine's reins around a branch on a fallen stump. "Dad has hunted 'em before. He knows."

"I see." She glanced toward Ryan, who handed over the sleeping bag without a word, his silence further baffling her. "Thanks."

With skill born of experience—she'd been known to camp on her own property when she needed to escape—Dani unrolled, then unzipped the bag, spreading it on the snow like a blanket, waterproof side down, flannel side up. On this cozy, insulated covering she now spread their lunch.

Sawyer ate with enthusiasm. Ryan, Dani noted, nibbled for a bit before his appetite seemed to kick in and he consumed a man-size share. About the time he swallowed his last bite, he seemed to relax a little, and even managed a smile of sorts.

What *is* his problem? Dani wondered, by now feeling a little foolish and unwanted. Had she unwittingly intruded on what Ryan had hoped would be father-son time? Undoubtedly, she realized, wishing she'd stayed home. A need to be close had driven her to butt in on their togetherness. She did not belong here. She was not part of this family unit.

"What's next?"

Sawyer's question sliced into her gloom. "Excuse me?"

"What do you do next at a picnic in the snow?" The boy said the words as if she were a dunce or hard-of-hearing.

"Sawyer...." Ryan's tone warned his son, who was obviously feeling his oats, to cool it.

Immediately, he did. "I just wondered."

"Then I'll just tell you," Dani answered, trying to think up something quick. On sudden inspiration, she got to her feet and began to search the ground. Sawyer was beside her in a heartbeat, copying her every move even though he couldn't possibly know what they sought.

Finally, he gave up. "What are we looking for?"

"A couple of rocks," she told him. "About this big." She formed a circle the size of a quarter with her thumb and forefinger.

"Try over there," Ryan suggested to Sawyer, pointing to where the ground had been protected from snow somewhat by the branches of a pine tree.

Sawyer hurried over and in seconds shouted with glee. "I've found some!" He showed them to Dani. "So what are you going to do with them?"

"*I'm* not doing anything," she said. "*You* are. Those rocks, young man, are your snowman's eyes."

"My...?" He caught his breath, eyes sparkling as her idea sank in. "Yeah. I'll make the biggest snowman in the whole wide world!"

Laughing, Dani walked back to the sleeping bag and started to sit on the spot she'd vacated moments earlier. Just as she did, Ryan grabbed her arm and tugged, an action that sent her sprawling...right across his lap.

"What are you doing?" she demanded, trying to get off him.

"I want you closer than that," he replied.

Dani stilled her struggle and sat back on her heels, her face mere inches from Ryan's. "Do you, Ryan? Do you?"

"Of course I do," he answered, clearly baffled by her intensity. "Don't you believe me?"

"Frankly, no."

"Why the hell not?"

"Because a mere five minutes ago you were giving me a very cold shoulder," Dani snapped.

For a moment, Ryan looked as if he were going to deny it, then he gave her a sheepish shrug. "I admit I wasn't glad to see you when you first rode up."

"Thanks a million."

"It's not the way it sounds, Dani."

"Then what way is it?"

He hesitated as though he had something to confess, but didn't want to. "You, um, get to me. It's...frustrating."

Totally without a clue as to what he was trying to say, Dani could only shake her head in bewilderment. "What *are* you talking about?"

Instead of answering, Ryan glanced over her shoulder. Dani turned to find out what he was looking at and saw Sawyer, with his back to them, engrossed in rolling the base for his snowman. She once again faced her companion, who never shifted his gaze off his son. "What are you talking about, Ryan?"

"This," he growled, taking her hand, laying it on his bulging fly. "I'm talking about this."

Though Dani knew Sawyer wasn't watching—and wouldn't see if he did look, thanks to her position—she jerked her hand back as if Ryan were red-hot. That thought, so true in a way, hit home all at once and Dani couldn't stop the laughter that bubbled up inside.

"This ain't funny, lady."

"I know," she agreed, instantly ceasing the amusement that was probably more a result of her discomfiture than anything else. She avoided Ryan's piercing gaze for a second, then intercepted it. "I'm sorry I laughed."

"You should be, and, just for the record, you'll pay."

Dani tensed. "What do you mean?"

"I mean, there'll come a time...soon...when you're wanting me as bad as I want you."

His threat, spoken with tender confidence, was potent as an aphrodisiac. She caught her breath and looked away, instantly on fire for him and close to being consumed by it. "I do now."

He groaned. She sighed. He leaned to one side and patted a spot on the sleeping bag, a good yard away. "Sit."

"Way over there?"

He nodded. "Unless you want to participate in a live demonstration of the birds-and-bees facts I gave Sawyer last night?"

With a gulp and shake of her head, Dani sat where he pointed. Silence prevailed for a good five minutes, during which they watched Sawyer create his snowman. Her eyes, but not her thoughts, thus engaged, Dani couldn't help thinking about what had just transpired between her and Ryan—the blatant honesty, the mutual desire. She'd never experienced anything quite the same. She wasn't sure how she felt about it.

"I hope you know I'm not usually this... this *free* with men," she murmured for lack of a better word, suddenly feeling a little self-conscious.

"Does that mean you think I'm special?"

"Yes, though why I can't say," Dani continued in her bewilderment. "I mean, I barely know you...." Her voice trailed to silence as the enormity of last night's encounter hit home. In her mind's eye, she saw the two of them in the bathroom, in the dark, just as they'd been last night. It was as if some other woman stood there with Ryan, kissing and touching, being kissed and touched in return. *Oh, God.*

"I can remedy that," Ryan said with a laugh, apparently not in the least bit insulted by her tactless comment, even though he had every right to be. "What do you want to know about me?"

"Everything," Dani replied. "Starting with where you were born."

"Wyoming."

Dani gaped at him. "I thought you were an Okie."

"No. But my mother was, which is why she moved back to Oklahoma when she and my dad split."

"Do you have family in Wyoming?"

"My father, his current wife and some stepsiblings is all."

She heard unmistakable bitterness. "Do you ever see them?"

"No... we don't get along."

"May I ask why?" Dani wasn't sure why she pushed. Normally, she wasn't so nosey.

Ryan hesitated a millisecond before he shrugged. "Because the bastard let my mother take me away and never once tried to get me back."

"I'm sorry, Ryan," she said, touching his arm to comfort him.

He shrugged off her touch. "It's old news. I'm over it."

"Of course," she murmured without an ounce of conviction. The man had just admitted he didn't get along with his parent. He called that "over it"? Ryan gave her a hard look as though reading her thoughts. Dani ignored him. "So how did you like Oklahoma?"

"Well enough to find work there as a ranch hand as soon as I was old enough. I moved right out of my mom's place into a bunkhouse. You can pretty much figure out the rest of the story from there, I guess."

Figure out what happened all the years between teenage and— Suddenly realizing she didn't have a clue how old Ryan was, Dani frowned. What she knew about this man could be written on the head of a pin with space left over. As for figuring everything out, well, she couldn't begin to do that. She didn't know him well enough.

Didn't know him well enough. Didn't know him at all…a situation an afternoon's or even a day's worth of talking would not remedy, since what she needed to learn about this man were truths that mere words could never reveal.

Yet she'd agreed to meet him for a midnight seduction.

Dani's blood ran cold at the thought. How easily she'd fallen prey to his sweet talk, his skilled touch, his kisses. Had she really learned nothing from her years in the school of hard knocks? Or had fate cruelly sent her the one-in-a-million cowboy who could do it to her again?

"Anything else you want to know?" Ryan's question made Dani jump. He laughed and shook his head. "Where have you been?" he asked, no doubt referring to her wayward thoughts.

How could she tell him that a simple stroll down memory lane had left her stranded in a private hell? Abruptly, Dani came to life, gathering up the picnic things, stuffing them into the backpack.

Ryan hesitated for only a moment, then helped her, a look of puzzlement on his face.

"Dani! Dad! Look!"

Dani did and saw that Sawyer had virtually completed his snowman. "Where's his nose?"

Sawyer frowned at his masterpiece. "I don't have a carrot."

"Sure you do," Dani said, offering him one of the carrot slices she'd brought in their lunch.

"But that's not the right kind," the boy complained.

"Beggars can't be choosers," his dad retorted.

Beggars can't be choosers? Oh, yes, they could, Dani thought, coming to a sudden decision. At once, she squared her shoulders and erected an invisible, invincible wall between her and Ryan.

"Oh, all right." Grumbling with every step, Sawyer walked over and got the carrot stick from Dani. Seconds later, he stuck it in place on the snowman's face.

"It's perfect," Dani said. The next instant, she tucked the last of the picnic into the pack, stood and reached down to tug on the sleeping bag. "Up, Ryan. Picnic's over. I have to get back to the house."

He questioned her without words, but only for a heartbeat before he scrambled to his feet and grasped two corners of the unzipped sleeping bag. Dani grabbed the other two corners, and after shaking off the snowflakes that clung to it, they folded, zipped and rolled the bag until it was a compact bundle. That simple task, oddly intimate, shook

Dani so badly that she could barely function. But Ryan, busy securing the bag behind Sunshine's saddle, didn't seem to notice.

"Are you leaving?" Sawyer demanded, running up to tug on Dani's jacket.

"Uh-huh," she told him. "Now that I've finally finished the wedding gown, I have to catch up on all the household chores I've been neglecting."

"Can you spare the time to ride the borders of your place and check the fences with us?" Ryan asked. He stood by the high-strung palomino, rubbing the animal's neck as though attempting to win his trust.

He needn't have worried on that score, Dani couldn't help thinking. He obviously handled horses as well as he did women.

"I could," she replied, "but I don't think I will. I'm, uh, kind of cold." *And I don't want to lie outright about the borders.*

"So am I," said Sawyer, showing them his hands, beet-red from contact with the snow.

"Oh my goodness," Dani murmured, reaching out to rub some warmth back into the boy's fingers. "What you need is gloves." She glanced at Ryan's hands, also rather red, noting how large and capable they looked. Though he could lay claim to a callus or two, on the whole his hands were amazingly smooth for the type of work he did, the truth of which her body could vouch for. Dani gulped. "Why don't you two come back to the house with me now? I'll see if I can rustle up a pair of gloves for each of you."

"You've got gloves that will fit me?" Ryan held up his hands for her inspection, fingers splayed.

Remembering how wonderful those fingers felt when they caressed her breasts, Dani had to look away. Tomorrow, she reminded herself. He'll be gone by tomorrow... Tuesday at the latest. Surely...*surely*...she could resist him until then.

"I believe my ex left a pair in the tack room. He was about your size." Dani slipped her arms through the straps on the backpack, then gathered up Sunshine's reins, her movements as jerky and awkward as she suddenly felt.

Ryan said not a word, just looked at her, his face a study in speculation. When she moved to mount the palomino, he automatically assisted as any cowboy would, then stepped out of the way. For long moments, they stared at one another, neither speaking. Could he tell things had changed? she wondered. Did he realize how determined she was to save herself?

Did he understand there would be no midnight tryst?

"Why don't you and Sawyer go on," Ryan murmured. "I have some things I need to do before I head in."

"But your hands—"

He laughed shortly and hooked his thumbs through his belt loops, a move that pushed his jacket open and back, revealing a tantalizing length of torso, tooled-leather belt and faded denim. "My hands have been through a lot worse than a Colorado winter."

"Such as...?"

"An Oklahoma summer." He turned to Sawyer. "Mount up, son. You're going with Dani."

"But I want to go with you."

"I'll come back to the house in about an hour. You can go out with me again when I do."

Though Sawyer looked as if he'd love to argue, he wisely didn't. "Yes, sir." In seconds, the boy retrieved Tonto and stepped up into the saddle. "You *promise* I can go out with you this afternoon?"

"I promise," Ryan said, patting the Appaloosa on the rump, and his son on the thigh.

With an *adios* nod, Dani urged the palomino into a trot. Sawyer did the same, and moments later, the two of them disappeared down the trail leaving Ryan nothing more than troubled thoughts and a coldhearted snowman for company.

Yep. She'd gone and done it.

Ryan didn't know how, exactly—certainly couldn't remember when. But Dani had nonetheless managed to carve herself a niche in a heart that should have been solid as stone, thanks to years of hardening.

Damn, Ryan thought, frowning at the fencerow alongside which his horse trotted.

And that wasn't even the worst of it. Now that she'd nicked him, now that he was wounded, she apparently thought better of her attack and had retreated. At least, that's what he *thought* had happened. In truth, Ryan knew nothing more than that she was searing-hot one second, ice-cold the next.

So, was his wound mortal? Ryan thought for a moment, then decided that it wasn't. After all, he'd just met the woman on Thursday. And while not exactly a wizard, he wasn't an idiot either, and so didn't believe in any of that love-at-first-sight crap that television and the movies spouted.

No...*disappointed* was a word that better described his feelings because Ryan knew, beyond a shadow of a doubt, that there would be no rendezvous tonight and, therefore, no midnight magic.

Dani had saved herself from him—a damn good thing since he obviously wasn't capable of the self-denial required to do right by her. In the nick of time, she had glimpsed the future or remembered the past or *something* and come to her senses. Her gods smiled down on her while his . . . *his* . . . laughed their heads off at him.

And what did the future now hold for him? Why, exactly what it held Christmas Eve. No more. No less. Well, not much less. There was that missing chip of heart, but it would only hurt for a while.

"Dad! Dad!"

Sawyer burst out the door the minute Ryan exited the barn, where he'd just left Ali Baby. The boy's eyes shone with excitement about something. His grin stretched across the width of his young face. Ryan grinned back, wondering what had so excited his son.

"Whoa, there!" Ryan caught Sawyer, who nearly stumbled in the snow. Both of them laughed, Sawyer's a bubble of joy that indicated something was definitely up. "What's cooking?"

"Dani's best friend's son, Ricky, wants me to come over and play for a couple of hours. Can I, Dad? Can I?" He spoke so fast the entire sentence sounded like one long word.

Ryan stood a moment letting the stream of words soak in and separate into a comprehensible message. "Dani's best friend?" He raised his gaze from his son, now clinging to him, eyes huge and pleading, to Dani, who walked slowly toward them from the house.

"Jonni Maynard," she said with a slight smile. "We go back clear to grade school. The friend I talked to on the phone the night you wound up in my trunk . . . ?"

Ryan vaguely remembered hearing about this *best* friend, Johnny, before. The last time, however, jealousy—cold and sharp as one of the icicles hanging from Dani's roof—had not stabbed at his heart. The sudden pain surprised and disconcerted him. "Um . . . how old is Ricky?"

"Seven and a half," Sawyer announced with authority.

"Jonni wants to pick Sawyer up in a half hour or so and then bring him back later." She shrugged. "Ricky's a real bundle of energy. I'm sure she needs a break."

"She? Johnny's a she?"

Dani gave him the oddest look, one he surely deserved for his blurted-out question. "Yes. Her name is J-o-n-n-i. Jonni Lisa Maynard."

"Oh." He felt the fool and found himself stammering like some tenderfoot to love. "I thought, not that it matters to me, of course, that your best friend was a, well, a man. It seemed a little—" Ryan's voice suddenly failed him, his intended sentence long forgotten when the phraseology of his thoughts suddenly registered.

Tenderfoot to love? *Love?*

"Sweet Sadie Sawbucks!"

"Sweet *what?*" Dani stared at him as though he'd lost his marbles, which he certainly had if the L-word had begun to invade his thoughts.

"Sadie Sawbucks," Ryan murmured, only belatedly realizing his answer had told Dani exactly nothing. "Sort of a non–curse word I once used." He shrugged. "Like you, the boss's wife didn't allow profanity—"

"I'm just trying to save your son's innocent ears."

"I know, and I'm trying to cooperate, just as I did years ago when me and several of the hands made up this phrase."

"What does it mean, exactly?"

"It, um, refers to a certain woman some of the men used to visit—"

"A lady of the night, perhaps?"

He grinned. "That's one way to put it, though she worked all hours."

"And Sawbucks was her last name?"

"No. A sawbuck is what she charged for her, um, favors."

"You're kidding!"

"Nope."

"My God. Did you ever drop in on her?"

"No, ma'am."

"You swear?"

"I do." He shook his head, bemused. "I haven't thought of those words in years. Don't know where they came from today."

"But you do know why you said them . . . ?" Dani wondered aloud.

"Oh yeah," he murmured, leaving it at that. Not for anything was he going to confess that the word *love* now hovered in his head, ready and waiting to intrude on his thoughts, his speech, and God forbid, his plans to tell her goodbye.

Chapter Seven

Though Ryan had serious doubts about spending hours alone with Dani, he agreed to let Sawyer go to Ricky's. Dani immediately went indoors to phone her friend, while Sawyer plopped down on one of the chairs on the side porch, by all appearances intending to wait outside until Jonni arrived to get him.

Ryan joined his son on the porch, where he delivered a gentle lecture on manners. Sawyer listened with obvious impatience, but said nothing until Ryan finished, when he said, "I already know this stuff."

"Yeah, well, I'm just making sure you *remember* it." Ryan stood and walked to the kitchen door in time to meet Dani, headed back outside. He braked. So did she. For a second they stared at one another, then he stepped aside, allowing her to exit. Dani, now wearing her jacket, brushed against him as she squeezed by, temptation on the move.

Ryan winced, shook his head and headed to the kitchen counter for a water glass, all the while marveling that so simple an encounter as that one could leave him so rattled, so primed.

Was it love? Was it?

Already?

God, but he hoped not. That's all he needed right now. . . stupid emotion to complicate his life, cloud his future when he didn't have time for it.

Not that he'd ever admit his feelings to Dani or otherwise play the fool. Ryan wouldn't. . . couldn't. He had Sawyer to think about—Sawyer, who deserved his total dedication and concentration for at least as many years as he'd been without it.

Ryan filled the glass from the tap, which ran icy cold in seconds. He drank the whole thing down in a couple of swallows, all the while listening to the murmur of voices outside. He heard Dani's laughter, then Sawyer's. They got along well, he reluctantly acknowledged, and even though they'd known each other less than three days, they shared an easy affection that could only grow if fed time and patience.

In short, loving Dani might not be such a bad thing for the boy.

So why did the thought of it scare Ryan half to death? Because what had transpired between them thus far defied logic, common sense and caution. Near strangers who had both loved before and no longer took chances, they had nonetheless kissed in the dark and tempted fate. He couldn't say why, couldn't yet say he regretted it. All he knew was that he'd enjoyed it way too much.

What was going on here? he wondered. A Christmas miracle? A little Yuletide magic? A gift from above he'd be a total idiot to deny?

"She's here! She's here!"

At the sound of Sawyer's cry of joy, Ryan glanced out the window and saw a gleaming black pickup truck parked in the driveway. Out bounced a red-haired, freckle-faced boy, who had to be Ricky. He fairly danced in his excitement to have a playmate for a while, as did Sawyer. Ryan marveled that there was no period of adjustment between the two boys, no awkwardness at all. Grinning like lifelong buddies, they piled into the truck and shut the door.

Realizing that Sawyer intended to leave without so much as a "see ya later," Ryan stepped out onto the porch. Putting his thumb and forefinger to his lips, he let loose with a shrill whistle that brought Dani, now on her way to the truck, to an instant halt.

Sawyer heard it, too, as Ryan had intended, and with a guilty start, threw open the truck door, dashed to the porch and hurled himself into Ryan's arms.

"I'll be back in just a little while," Sawyer murmured into his dad's shirt.

Ryan noted that he patted him on the back, much like adults sometimes did when they didn't know what else to do. "Good, because I'll be right here waiting."

Sawyer tipped back his head and grinned, accepting the promise as if he'd never been left alone or lied to, two things Ryan thought had happened too many times in his young life.

With renewed determination to keep things on an emotionally even keel at any cost, Ryan let Sawyer go. As the boy charged back to the truck, Ryan stared at the brunette seated behind the steering wheel. From what he could see, she looked petite in build and fragile as a feather. Did she really know what she was getting into? he wondered as Sawyer crawled into the cab and slammed the door.

As if reading his thoughts, Jonni Maynard looked Ryan's way and waved. He nodded in return, then watched as Dani and her friend talked for a moment through the open truck window. Ryan heard laughter—Jonni's—then, a second later, the truck began to roll down the driveway.

In seconds Dani stood there alone. She looked a little pink around the gills. Cold? he wondered. Or had friend Jonni said something to fluster her?

Probably the latter, he guessed when Dani would not meet his gaze. What married friend wouldn't tease a single one about a stranger of the opposite sex living in her house? Suddenly, Ryan realized how compromising their situation really was—even in the modern age. Would Dani's reputation be ruined in the community?

Impulsively, he descended the few steps of the porch and walked over to Dani, still rooted to the snow-patched spot.

"Are you okay?" he asked.

"Fine. Why?"

"Your cheeks are about the color of the icing on those cookies you baked for me."

"Really?" She put a hand to her cheek as if touching it could verify the truth of his words. "Must be chapped. Winter is so hard on my skin."

Yeah, right. "I hope your friend didn't get the wrong idea about us."

"Meaning . . . ?" As if she didn't know.

"You're not married. I'm not, either. We're sharing a roof."

"Oh, *that.*" Dani's blush deepened. "She did ask if you, er, if I, um, if *we*—" She sighed. "What I mean is, she did tease me a little, but only euphemistically, since the kids were listening. I set her straight quick, of course." Dani's gaze locked with his for the first time in a long time. Her chin tilted in defiance. "I mean, you are good-looking and all, and I am physically attracted, but I explained that you'll be leaving very soon and that anything we did would be mere momentary gratification and, therefore, pointless."

"I see. And she said . . . ?"

Dani hesitated then laughed with honest humor. "She said, 'You have exactly two hours. Get busy!'"

Ryan had to laugh, too, and felt considerably better for it. "So what *are* your plans for the next couple of hours, Ms. Sellica?"

"No plans . . . beyond avoiding rooms with doors that lock, that is." The look she gave him shot down any of his lingering, misguided hopes that they could spend the afternoon in the bathroom, or, since Sawyer was gone, in her bed. "Why?"

"I was thinking I'd tune up the truck. Want to help?"

She didn't answer right away, but glanced toward the garage, where her old truck waited. "I would like to learn how to take care of her."

"Then come on," Ryan said. "We'll finish this morning's little talk." He headed toward the garage.

Dani caught up with a hop, skip and a jump. "But I thought we already did," she said, panting, as she scurried to keep pace with his long strides.

"How could we, when I didn't get to ask anything?"

She gave him a startled glance. "You have questions?"

"Hundreds." Upon reaching the garage door, Ryan raised it so he could step into the shadowy building with its oil-stained concrete floor, shelf-lined walls and solitary window. He noticed that Dani didn't follow, but stood outside, eyeing him with real alarm.

"What, exactly, do you want to know?" she asked, a question that made him wonder absently what secrets she was keeping.

"The story of your life, of course," he answered. "And don't leave out a single juicy detail." Ryan opened the drivr's side door of the truck and motioned her to get inside the vehicle. She did with obvious reluctance. "Start the engine."

"I don't have the key." She moved as though to go fetch it. Ryan stopped her with an upraised hand.

"Stay put. I'll go." He took two steps, then halted and turned back to her. "Where do you keep it, anyway?"

"On the wall hook just inside the kitchen door," she said.

With a nod, Ryan left, leaving Dani alone. She stared after him for a moment, then groaned and rested her forehead on the steering wheel of her faithful vehicle. "What am I doing out here?" she demanded aloud. It didn't really matter that there was no one there to reply. Dani already knew the answer, and it wasn't good.

She now sat alone in her garage for one reason, and one reason only—she wanted to be around Ryan. Never mind that the pain of his impending departure would correspond directly to how much time she spent with him. Dani simply could not bear the thought of his working out here while she worked in the house.

It was that simple.

She suddenly remembered Jonni's response to her first sight of Ryan standing on the porch. Her friend had said so much more than Dani had shared with her houseguest, not the least of which was a whispered, rather risqué suggestion of what they should do now that they had the house to themselves for a while. Dani blushed again, thinking about it. Jonni never had been one to mince words, and Jonni believed that Dani needed to get a life.

But was Ryan really "a life"? Or was he a walking, talking tragedy—a heartache waiting to happen?

Dani thought the latter and so scrambled from the truck.

"Get tired of waiting?" It was Ryan, already back with the key.

"I, um, just remembered something I had to do," Dani lied, moving toward the door.

Ryan blocked her exit. "It can't wait? I'm really good at this."

"Well..."

He stepped to the front of the truck and raised the hood, then peeked out around it, his smile fetching. "I could teach you a lot, and it won't take long."

I'll just bet. "I really need to leave." As in *now!*

His face fell. "Oh."

Ryan's disappointment appeared so keen. Dani groaned inside and struggled to resist his pleading, puppy-dog eyes. "Well, maybe I could stay for a few minutes."

He positively beamed at her. "Here," he said, tossing her the keys.

Dani caught them, then climbed into the truck. "Tell me when."

"Now."

With a twist of the wrist, she started the engine. While it chugged, she sat in silence, mentally kicking herself in the backside for her inability to resist the man. What was it? she wondered. His eyes? His smile? His body?

Try all of the above, her libido sassily replied.

"Okay, kill it."

Dani did and got out of the truck, walking to where Ryan bent over the engine, fiddling with something out of sight. His tush, molded in denim, begged to be touched. She tucked her hands into her pockets to keep them in line, belatedly realizing that Ryan now looked back at her and had surely noticed her fascination with that part of his anatomy.

Darn!

"Would you hand me a screwdriver?"

"Flat or Phillips?"

"Flat."

She did as requested, watching while he popped a frayed belt from some part of the engine. He then reached for one of the spare belts always kept on hand, and removed the cardboard wrapping. He grinned at Dani, from the look of things glad to have her around while he worked. It triggered a memory.

"Actually, this isn't the first time I've helped a guy in a garage," Dani told Ryan.

"No?"

"No. I once had a boyfriend who worked on his car every spare second. If I wanted to see him at all, I had to hang out where he did—a smelly old garage much like this one."

Ryan laughed.

"I tried really hard to distract him from that darned junker of his. Unfortunately, I never managed to."

"Must not have been using the right bait." He stepped back. "Start her up again when I tell you to."

With a nod, Dani walked to the driver's side and slipped behind the wheel again, leaving the door open. "Ready?"

"Not yet." Several minutes passed. "Now!"

Dani started the engine.

"Okay," Ryan called. "That's got it."

Though Dani knew she should ask just what was got, she didn't. Who cared about that when there were more important questions that needed asking. "What bait is the right bait? Apple pie? A fishing rod? The swimsuit issue of *Sports Illustrated?*"

"No to all three," Ryan replied from right beside her, wiping his hands clean on a shop towel.

"Then what?"

"You." He tossed the towel to a table and ducked his head to look into the truck at her, his hands resting on the roof of the vehicle. "You, Dani."

Handsome as the devil himself, Ryan now stood very close. With a groan of defeat, Dani lifted her face and accepted the kiss he gave her. It wasn't enough for either of them, of course, and after a few seconds' maneuvering, she found herself prone on the seat of the truck, Ryan full on top of her.

Though this model truck sported an uncommonly wide bench seat, Dani knew that Ryan couldn't possibly fit his six-foot-plus length on it. Nonetheless, she didn't worry much about the picture they made—two adults in such a compromising situation, feet and legs dangling out the open door. Instead, she focused on the joy of his weight, the warmth of his body, the magic of his caress.

He kissed every millimeter of her face, thoroughly and gently, as if he was a man who had all of eternity to get it done. Dani returned his kisses full measure and more. So good, she thought. So right.

He touched her. She touched him. Button by button, snap by snap, in slow motion, they tempted self-control... until Ryan suddenly raised onto his elbows and looked her straight in the eye.

"Are you sure, Dani?"

Cold air swirled where his body had been, chilling her flesh. "About what?"

"Us, of course. You do understand I'm leaving tomorrow, or, at the latest, Tuesday?"

Dani nodded. "That's the plan."

"Then why are you letting me do this?"

"For the same reason you're letting me, cowboy." Irritated with him for having the good sense to question their folly, Dani put her palms on his bare chest and pushed. "Let me up, Ryan."

"Yes, ma'am." It took two full minutes to untangle, rearrange and settle in, but finally Ryan sat behind the steering wheel in the truck driver's spot with Dani as passenger. "Sorry about that," he muttered as he raised his butt and stuffed the tail of his just-rebuttoned shirt back into his jeans. "I didn't lure you into the garage to attack. I just wanted... wanted—"

"That *is* the key word, here, isn't it?" Dani interjected. "'Wanted'?"

Ryan nodded. "But what I want and what you want couldn't possibly be the same."

"I'm not so sure about that." Dani, clothes now secure and in place, half turned in the seat and leaned back on the door. She said nothing for a moment, then softly asked, "What *do* you want, Ryan?"

"To get close to you for a little while." He stared off into space for a moment, clearly disconcerted about something. "I've got a lot on my plate, Dani. Reclaiming my truck, finishing my move to Wyoming, getting Sawyer enrolled in school, finding my ranch. It wouldn't be fair to tell you I'm looking for any sort of permanent hookup, because I'm not. I'm just not."

"Well, hold on to your hat," she replied. "Because *neither am I.*"

"That's bull and you know it."

"But—"

"But nothing," he said. "There's not a woman alive in this world who doesn't want a rock-solid relationship with someone. Oh, they may deny it, like you're doing, but deep inside they want it all. So do most men, now that I think about it."

His philosophizing surprised her, even though she'd caught glimpses of his sensitivity before. "Including you?"

"Sure, including me. Unfortunately, I've got a son to see after, so any need of mine is secondary to his."

Finally. . . the crux of the matter. "And I have no such priorities."

"Exactly!" He beamed at her, obviously relieved that she understood what he was trying to say.

"You think you're so smart," Dani snapped, suddenly angry with him. "Lumping all women together, analyzing their motives like some high-paid shrink. Well, I'm here to say you don't know a darn thing about the opposite sex—me, most of all."

Ryan's jaw dropped.

"Have I told you about Mick, my ex-husband?"

"Apparently not enough."

"Mick and I met at a rodeo. He was one of the competitors—a team roper." She flicked a glance at Ryan, who had the muscular build of just such a competitor. "Ever done that?"

He pointed to his ornate silver belt buckle. Dani leaned over for a better look and saw enough to confirm what she'd already guessed: at some point in time, this cowboy had won cash and a belt buckle for his skill in wrestling steers to the ground.

"Surprise, surprise," she murmured somewhat caustically.

"Nationals, three years ago."

"Of course." She didn't speak for a moment—silently ruing her knack for picking them out.

"Go on," Ryan immediately urged.

Dani heaved a sigh and complied. "Mick was a looker—tall with a great body. I flipped over him. Just flipped. We were married in three months. Divorced in eighteen. But in that short time, he managed to destroy my reputation as a rancher, alienate my friends and sell the timber rights of my land to my stepfather, who had no right to them."

"I believe you said your stepfather got half your land when your mother died . . . ?"

"That's right. He wanted it all, of course, and had mother not died so suddenly, probably would've found a way to sweet-talk her out of it. That was the plan when he married her, you know—to get our ranch, our land."

Ryan said nothing for a moment, clearly lost in thought. His frown said he'd noticed there were important details missing from her tale—namely, the amount of her wealth and size of her ranch, prime motivators for Mick's and her stepfather's treachery. Still, she could not open up. Ryan knew too well how susceptible she was to cowboys—and not because she'd told him moments earlier. No, he had seen her turn to putty at a word, a touch. He truly understood the magnitude of her gullibility.

"Surely you didn't let them get away with it?"

"Only for as long as it took me to find a lawyer. I won the case, of course. Mick had forged my signature on the papers, pure and simple."

"And what happened to him and your stepfather?"

"Why, nothing, thanks to the fact that they have friends in high places. No, the worst that happened to Mick was that no one around here would hire him. As for dear old stepdad, he's still around, though I think he lost respect and, naturally, power."

"And the point of all this?"

He didn't know? Good grief! "To prove to you that all women are not looking for long-term relationships. I'll never be able to trust another man enough to turn my life over to him."

"So who's asking you to do that? Most men want a partner, Dani, not a peon."

"Not in my experience." She huffed her weariness with the whole conversation. "The bottom line is this—I'm not averse to just having a few hours' fun with you."

"Oh yeah . . . ?"

"Or maybe I should say *wasn't.* Talking about Mick has definitely put a damper on my spirit of adventure. At the moment, I'd rather vacuum or dust or scrub the toilet or something."

"Thanks a million," muttered Ryan, justly insulted.

"Oh, it's not *you,*" she hastily assured him.

"No, it's a long-gone cowboy who should be long forgotten. He was an outlaw, you know. All us cowpokes don't take advantage of all you cowgirls."

"Sure you don't." She reached for the door handle, only to halt when Ryan grabbed her other hand.

"I'd never hurt you, Dani. Never."

I'm going to die when you leave.

"I owe you too much. You took me and my boy in. You fed us, sheltered us, made Christmas extra special. I wasn't lying when I said I'd never forget it. I really won't."

"I won't forget you, either, I don't think," she murmured, a partial lie. She didn't "think," she *knew* he'd haunt her for eternity. He'd be the cowboy who got away, that special someone against whom all others would forever pale in comparison.

The crunch of frozen gravel on the driveway alerted them to Jonni's return.

Clearly startled, Ryan reached over and turned Dani's wristwatch so he could see the time.

"Damn, already?" he murmured, getting out of the truck, and ducking back under the hood to get on with his tune-up.

Her spirits lower than the temperature, Dani walked out to greet Jonni, who looked as if she'd survived the boys' trial playtime well enough.

"How was he?" Dani asked with a nod to Sawyer, now headed to the garage with both Ricky and Ricky's little sister at his heels.

"The perfect gentleman." Jonni grinned. "How was *he?*"

"Still a mystery, I'm afraid," Dani replied with honest regret. Sure she was relieved she hadn't really made love with the man, but only ninety-nine percent so. There was still that one percent sick with disappointment.

"Are you telling me you didn't take advantage of the fact that you had two whole hours to yourselves?"

"We didn't sleep together, if that's what you're asking," Dani replied.

"Sleep, my foot. I wanted you to have sex with the guy, Dani. You do remember what that is, don't you? Sex? Where you and a man get naked, find a bed or a wall, and—"

"I remember the steps," Dani interjected dryly.

"Yet you didn't do it." Jonni shook her head in obvious disbelief. "Why, for Pete's sake? This cowboy is perfect for your particular situation."

"And what situation is that?"

"Once bitten, twice shy. Ryan Given is temporary with a capital *T*, which means he has no designs on your ranch, just your body. I'm talking guilt-free, fear-free fun—providing you practice safe sex, of course."

Dani thought about her words for several seconds before she spoke, her words earnest and probing. "You talk a good game, but if you were me, would you really, I mean *really,* get close to any ol' cowboy you've only known since Thursday night?"

Jonni opened her mouth to reply, but never said a word before the sound of children's laughter emanated from the garage. The women glanced toward the door in time to see Ryan, Sawyer and Ricky spill out of the building. On Ryan's shoulders perched Pattie, squealing enjoyment of the ride. The deep rumble of his laughter, the twinkle in his eyes were enough to make Dani's stomach flip-flop and her heart shift into overdrive.

"Any ol' cowboy?" Jonni murmured, reminding Dani she'd just asked her friend a question. "No. But *this* good-looking, hardworking, born-to-be-a-daddy cowboy? You bet your sweet—"

"Mom! Mom! Lookit me!" Pattie held on to her mount with a handful of his hair. Though it had to hurt, Ryan just chuckled and headed around the yard, bouncing her as though he were her bucking bronco. Pattie hung on, laughing like crazy.

"Want me to borrow Sawyer for another couple of hours?" Jonni asked sotto voce, never taking her eyes off Ryan.

"How about for the whole night?" Dani countered, the next instant coming to her senses. "Just joking. I have good reasons for not getting involved with him, Jonni."

"Well, whatever they are, they can't be good enough."

Jonni's words, spoken with utmost sincerity, cut Dani to the heart. "You're serious, aren't you?"

"Absolutely."

"But you don't even know him."

"No, I don't. There's just something about that man, something that tells me I can trust him. Surely you feel it, too?"

Dani didn't reply for a moment, overcome with the truth of her old friend's words. She did feel *something* and was so glad since that explained why she'd let Ryan get so close, so fast. It didn't have anything to do with her morals or lack thereof. It had to do with him—his history, his character, his style. Other things mattered, too, among them looks, personality and work ethic. Then there was his son.

In combination, all of these ingredients yielded a fascinating product, and she'd be less than a woman if she wasn't tempted to try it. But did this necessarily mean she trusted him? Dani wasn't so sure.

"Whoa, horsey!" At Jonni's order, Ryan halted his trot, and with a grin, headed toward the passenger side of the truck. He lifted Pattie from his shoulders and, opening the truck door, deposited her into the cab with her mother.

Peering at him through the driver's side window, Dani noted that he was barely winded.

"Ricky? Where are you?" Jonni called through the window.

At once her son and Sawyer appeared around the corner of the garage, where they'd vanished on exiting the building moments earlier.

"Are we leaving?" Ricky's crestfallen expression said he had other plans.

"We are," his mother replied with a jerk of her head motioning him into the truck.

"Aw, heck." The boy, shoulders slumped, walked obediently to the truck and got in beside his sister. Ryan shut the vehicle door and stepped back. Jonni touched her finger to a button, rolling down the window on his side, as if wanting to make him feel included.

"Thanks for everything, you two," she said, glancing from Dani, on the left of the truck, to Ryan, on the right.

"Actually, we should thank you," Ryan replied, hastily adding, "Sawyer and me, that is." His gaze met Dani's through the window. She felt her face flame. "I know he had a good time."

Jonni smiled at him, then turned to Dani. "Are you coming to the meeting tomorrow night?"

"What meeting?" Dani asked.

"The road meeting. Seven o'clock. My place. Didn't I tell you?"

"You did not."

Jonni groaned. "Would you believe that's why I phoned you in your car Christmas Eve?" She shook her head, clearly dismayed that she'd forgotten the purpose of the call. "Everyone in the area is coming...everyone with a gripe about these awful county roads, that is. The plan is to form a committee and present our complaints to the Transportation Department. The way I see it, if we band together, they won't be able to ignore us the way they do when we try to tackle the problem individually."

"The roads are a mess, aren't they?" Dani murmured. "Sure, I'll come."

Jonni shifted her gaze to Ryan. "You're welcome, too, Ryan, and bring Sawyer. He can keep Ricky and Pattie occupied."

"Oh, Ryan probably won't be around." Dani could barely say the painful words. "I mean, he'll surely have his things back by then, and I know he's anxious to get on the road to Wyoming."

Jonni just shook her head and then a finger at Ryan. "You're crazy to choose Wyoming over Colorado. Why, apart from a few lousy roads, this stretch of country is perfect, just perfect."

"I can only agree with that," Ryan said softly, words that reminded Dani why she couldn't quite trust him. For all she'd learned about the man in the short time they'd been together, there was that much more that remained a riddle. And she'd learned the hard way how drawn she was to men of mystery.

Did he really intend to go to Wyoming? He'd claimed so from day one and she'd believed him, yet just now he sounded as if he could be convinced to stay in Colorado. Did that mean he was changing his mind about leaving? And if so, why?

The biggest part of Dani feared she was the reason.

But a secret part of her *hoped* she was.

Chapter Eight

Sawyer couldn't stop talking about Ricky for the rest of the afternoon. During supper he continued the narrative, describing in minute detail the boy's room, his toys, his house. He also reported on the habits of Ricky's parents, his little sister and his pets, among them goldfish, a cat, a dog and a gerbil.

Dani watched Ryan as his son chattered on, noticing his thoughtful expression and the way he hung on the boy's every word. It was almost as if the man took enough notes to fill a book. Dani guessed it would be a *how to,* a book to which he'd refer when stumped for inspiration on raising his child right.

Thankful that Sawyer's words obviated the need for mealtime small talk, Dani let her thoughts wander to when she, too, had tried to glean hints for success and happiness from the experts. It was just after her wedding. She'd watched her married friends closely, filing away for future reference this or that method of dealing with a household crisis. She'd learned a lot and tried to apply the jewels of wisdom to her own marriage, rocky from the beginning in spite of everything she did.

Dani remembered when, in a last-ditch effort to save her marriage, she'd actually considered pregnancy as a possible *glue* to mend the torn relationship. Thank goodness Mick had nixed the idea, no doubt because he knew he was going to move on. If he hadn't, she'd be in Ryan's shoes now—a single parent, struggling to do things right.

Tick...tick...tick....

In one of the sudden silences that sometimes fall on conversations, Dani heard clearly the clock on the kitchen wall. She winced, reminded that her own biological timepiece ticked as loudly. Regret that she had not argued with Mick washed over her, for she knew she would have loved her baby even if that no-good cowboy had fathered it. Resolutely squashing a sudden panic that she'd never have another chance, Dani told herself that it was not too late. She would love again.

Maybe loved now.

Dani caught her breath at the sudden thought, a sound so loud that Ryan and Sawyer both looked at her in surprise.

"Did you swallow a chicken bone or something?" This came from Sawyer, his expression as puzzled as his dad's.

"Or something," Dani smoothly lied. "I remembered that I was going to make a chocolate cake and got so busy I completely forgot."

"You can make it tomorrow." Sawyer's hopeful suggestion earned him a glare from Ryan. Quickly the boy added, "I'll help," as if he thought that would make everything better.

"We may be leaving tomorrow," Ryan said, words that were no comfort to Dani tonight. "We'll certainly be outta here by Tuesday."

Outta here? He sounded as if he couldn't wait to shake the dust—or was it snow?—of her place off his boots. That hurt. That really hurt. An amazing reaction considering that earlier that afternoon she'd worried that he'd set his sights on her ranch and wasn't going to leave.

Clearly, she needed some think time to get her head straight. One instant she wanted Ryan to go, the next she wondered if she might be head over heels in love with him. And then there was that constant ticktocking of her biological clock—an irritating background noise she'd been vaguely aware of before Ryan's arrival, but now, for some reason, could not ignore.

"I don't want to go."

Sawyer's words startled Dani. She shifted her gaze to Ryan to check his reaction.

"It'll be hard to leave Dani, won't it?" the cowboy murmured. "But maybe, when we get our own place, she can come for a visit."

"And bring Ricky?"

"Yeah, sure." Ryan looked a bit relieved. No doubt, Dani guessed, because he realized Ricky—not Dani—was the main reason Sawyer wanted to stay.

She felt another stab of hurt and, suddenly irritated with herself and the two of them, abruptly scooted back her chair. "If you guys don't mind, I'm going to excuse myself from the table. I've got some things I must do—"

"You mean, bake that cake?"

"She does not."

"—if we're going to drive into town tomorrow." She turned to Ryan. "You two are going into Clearwater with me, aren't you? I have to take Barb's dress to her."

"We're going. I want to talk to Chief Meeks about my truck."

"Good." She gave them a forced smile. "Then I guess I'll see you both in the morning." That said, Dani deposited her plate in the kitchen sink and headed out the door and down the hall to the haven of her bedroom.

But tonight, she found no peace there, a truth she blamed on the chaos of her thoughts, not the usually cozy room. Dani turned in early, slept fitfully and dreamed nonsense. She then rose late, having overslept once she'd finally nodded off.

To her surprise, Ryan and Sawyer were already in the kitchen, frying sausage and baking refrigerator biscuits. They grinned when she stumbled into the room, bleary-eyed and decidedly tousled of hair. Her ratty blue bathrobe just added to what must be a sad picture of charm and grace.

"Well, if it isn't Sleeping Beauty," Ryan commented. "Are you awake. . . or just sleepwalking?"

"She's got to be sleepwalking," Sawyer replied, getting into the mood of the moment. "The handsome prince hasn't kissed her yet."

"Then you'd better hop to it." Reaching out, Ryan gave his son a firm push in Dani's direction.

Sawyer shook his head and backed away, clearly disgusted at the thought. "I'm not the prince, Dad. You are."

"Me?"

"You." It was Sawyer's turn to shove, and he did, urging Ryan toward Dani, who just glared at them.

"I'm not so sure she wants to wake up." Ryan stepped close to Dani and framed her face with his hands. "Do you, Princess?"

"Yes, but I'm thinking a cup of coffee would work better," she said, tensing, capturing his wrists in her hands.

"There's no coffee in fairy tales," Sawyer interjected with a shake of his head.

"The expert has spoken," Ryan said as he touched his lips to Dani's forehead.

"Oh, Dad," Sawyer groaned. "That's not the right kind of kiss."

"No?" Ryan murmured with a glance in his son's direction. He did not release Dani and still stood so close she couldn't bring his features into focus.

"No. You have to do it on her mouth."

"Ah." Ryan looked back at Dani, his eyes glowing. Slowly, he lowered his head until his mouth covered hers. Though Dani expected a brief, brushing caress, what she got was one heck of a kiss—the toe-curling, mind-boggling, feel-it-to-the-bone kind. An I-don't-care-if-the-kid-is-watching kiss that was the wake-up call to end all wake-up calls.

You're in love, Danielle Sellica. In love.

The realization came so loud and clear that Dani thought she might've said the words aloud. Horrified, she jerked free of Ryan's embrace.

"Way to go, Dad!" Sawyer exclaimed, clapping his hands. "She's awake!"

Dead silence answered him.

"Dad?"

Abruptly, Ryan spun toward the stove. "Yes, she's awake...and just in time for sausage and biscuits. Hungry, Dani?"

With effort, Dani replied. "Not really."

"Good," Sawyer said. "That leaves more for me!" Those words, which he'd no doubt heard someone else say, earned him a look of censure from his dad, now headed to the table with a plate of breakfast. "I was just kidding."

"I should hope so." Ryan set the food on the table and glanced at Dani. "Coffee?"

"Yes, thanks...and maybe I'll have a biscuit, after all. That is, if you don't mind?" She glanced at Sawyer, who hung his head.

"I said I was just kidding," the boy repeated.

"I know," Dani replied with an honest laugh, reaching out playfully to tug a lock of his hair. God, but she'd miss him. The house would never be the same. Never.

And neither would she.

The three of them sat and, after grace was returned, began to eat. Dani marveled that they'd formed a routine so quickly. It was almost as if they were each part of a puzzle that was now complete. They fit together that well.

"I did the chores and then called the bank," Ryan said, words that made Dani glance at the clock. Nine o'clock. She really had overslept.

"And?"

"They told me what check last cleared, which was the last one I wrote, by the way. I told them to stop payment on all others until further notice."

"You were lucky."

"Yeah," he agreed with a solemn nod. "Now, if the truck will just be okay."

"We'll know soon." Too soon, to Dani's way of thinking.

An hour later found Ryan, Sawyer and Dani on the highway to Clearwater. Ryan thought back to the last time he'd traveled this particular stretch of road, headed the opposite way, of course—Christmas Eve, an eternity ago. He felt as if three other people had made that first trip. He marveled that he could have changed so much in such a short time and that he felt so differently about his son, his future, the driver... especially the driver.

To think he'd ever thought her bossy, stubborn and, God forbid, plain, when she was really the most yielding, flexible, sexy woman on the face of the earth. The opposite of Sawyer's mother, Erica, Dani provided him with no good reason to resist her charms beyond the fact that he wanted to devote himself to his son, who would not thank him for the effort. No, given the choice, Sawyer would probably sacrifice the ranch in Wyoming for a life in Colorado with Dani.

So much for using location as an excuse to ignore feelings he really needed to face up to and sort through. A better reason was that Dani had given him no indication, beyond lustful physical response, that she might be falling for him as hard as he seemed to be falling for her. In fact, there were times he wasn't at all sure she even liked the cowboy inside the willing body.

Better to move on as planned, he told himself as he stared out the window at the snow-blanketed hills and valleys. Better...and easier.

Clearwater bustled with Monday-morning-after-a-holiday activity. Dani dropped off Ryan and Sawyer at the police station, then drove to Barbara's house to deliver the gown she'd designed and created.

Since the wedding was planned for New Year's Day, Barb's house turned out to be as busy as Clearwater. From the looks of things, relatives had been arriving for days, resulting in a home filled with love and laughter. Naturally, Dani was treated again to all the funny stories of courtship, proposal and engagement, only this time they were presented from this or that aunt's and cousin's point of view.

Not for the first time, Dani envied Barb her big family—two brothers and three sisters—and her countless aunts, uncles, first-through-fourth cousins and grandparents. Then there were the in-laws...

So much noise. So much confusion. So much fun.

Dani thought of how quiet her house would be after Tuesday and almost cried. To make matters worse, Barb showed off all her wedding gifts and shared her honeymoon plans.

By the time Dani got away—a full two hours later—her spirits seemed to have found a permanent home in the heel of her boot. Blinking back tears, she drove to the police station, where she sat in her car for five whole minutes to gain control of her emotions.

Still a bit weepy, still down in the dumps, Dani finally went inside to find Ryan and Sawyer. She was directed to the lounge, where she discovered them seated at the break table, talking with Cliff. Ryan grinned when she walked in, and Dani could tell the news was good.

For him, anyway. It could only be bad for her... unless it would be a week or two before he could get his vehicle back.

"Did you see the truck?" Ryan asked.

She gulped back the knot in her throat. "You mean, it's here?"

"In the parking lot. You didn't see it?"

"No." Tears had a way of blinding.

"Would you believe that most of our things are still loaded in back of it?"

"Great." She tried to say the word with enthusiasm. Ryan's gaze narrowed, telling her she hadn't quite succeeded. Dani tried again. "I'm so happy for you, Ryan." To punctuate the words, she walked over and stood next to him, laying her arm across his wide shoulders in a brief hug.

To her surprise, Ryan turned slightly and put both arms around her waist, hugging her hard, an action not lost on Cliff, who arched one eyebrow but said nothing. "I feel like a new man, let me tell you."

Gently, Dani eased free. "Well, now that I've finally gotten rid of that wedding gown, I feel like a new woman."

"I think this calls for a celebration, don't you?" Ryan stood and turned to Cliff. "Lunch is on me."

"Sorry, I can't today," the police chief said. "Too many officers still off. But you three go on ahead and have a real nice time."

Ryan nodded and turned to Dani. "How does lunch at the Clearwater Café sound—after we find a bank that will take my ATM card, that is."

Dani faked a smile. "Lovely."

"Ready, sport?" Ryan tousled Sawyer's hair as he so often did, and, as usual, Sawyer endured the gesture without complaint.

"Ready." The boy stood, too, and after goodbyes and thanks to Cliff, the threesome walked out to the parking lot, where Dani's car waited . . . right next to a truck that turned out to be Ryan's.

"I can't believe you didn't see this truck," he commented.

"Of course I saw it," Dani retorted, perhaps a little too shortly. She noticed that Ryan's gaze narrowed again. "I just didn't know it was yours. Have you forgotten I've never seen your truck before?"

"I guess I had," he murmured, eyeing her with what could only be suspicion. Dani faked another smile. Not for anything would she let him find out that she thought she loved him. He had his life to live. She had hers. And even if she did love him, that was no promise that she could ever really trust him. Mick had done his work well.

"Shall we take two vehicles?" he asked.

"Why not leave yours here until after lunch. All your stuff will be safer."

"You have a point," Ryan murmured with a glance at the things loaded in the long bed of the huge white pickup truck.

The three of them piled into Dani's car and made the short drive to the café, which had cleared of some of the usual noontime crowd since it was now after one o'clock.

Over blue plate specials, Ryan filled her in on details of the truck theft she did not know, namely, the police theory that the convicts had used the loaded-down truck as part of their disguise. Ryan listed what had vanished—relatively few things—and bragged about what remained—Sawyer's Christmas present, a box of rodeo trophies, his stereo.

He then asked Dani about Barbara, and in a voice as bereft of emotion as she could manage, she told him all she knew of her friend's wedding and honeymoon plans. If Ryan heard the wistful note she could not control, he did not comment on it.

After a leisurely lunch, Dani, Ryan and Sawyer walked through downtown Clearwater, still decorated for Christmas. As always, Dani's heart swelled with love for the little town, place of her birth. The shops were quaint in a wonderful way, meeting needs in big-city style, yet charming all who shopped there.

Dani's favorite was an old-fashioned hardware store that boasted everything from mousetraps to cast-iron skillets to kerosene lanterns. Ryan and Sawyer fell in love with the place, and as a result, they spent over an hour checking out every nook and cranny.

That accomplished, they moved down the block to a corner drugstore, complete with soda fountain. There they sat on stools at a tall counter and indulged in chocolate sundaes, calling them belated desserts.

There was a very family feel about the whole afternoon, Dani thought as she ate. And she found herself wishing she could just latch on to Ryan and Sawyer forever. How easy life would be with this pair around to love and care for. Sawyer could catch the school bus every day. A child with his winning personality would have no problem fitting right in.

As for Ryan, he could take over running the ranch while she—

Take over running the ranch? *My God, am I* that *far gone?*

Apparently, Dani realized with some dismay.

"What do you think we should do now?" Ryan asked, breaking into her fog of self-recrimination and regret.

"We can always shop some more," she murmured. "We've only been down one side of the street."

Ryan grinned. "I mean about tonight. I know you're ready to be rid of your houseguests. I was thinking maybe Sawyer and I should just stay at the Garrett Motel, then be on our way tomorrow."

Dani's heart hit the linoleum floor. "Don't be silly. Your suitcases are at the ranch. You two should just stay with me, then leave from there."

"I don't know..."

"Aw, Dad, come on," Sawyer suddenly piped up. "I want to see Ricky at the meeting tonight. You said we could go."

Though Ryan clearly resisted the plan, he agreed with a nod. Dani, faced with reality, gave them both a weak smile.

"I don't know what I'm going to do without you guys around. It'll be quiet... too quiet... I think."

"You can always turn on the radio in the kitchen," commented Sawyer, who looked a little sad, himself.

"So I can," Dani replied. "Which reminds me that I need a new radio."

"I saw some on a shelf over there," Sawyer said, pointing to the far side of the drugstore.

"Why don't you pick one out for me?" Dani could see he was getting restless, but didn't dare eat her ice cream any faster lest she get a headache.

"Okay." With a leap off the stool and a bound in the direction of the radios, Sawyer vanished around a row of shelves.

"What's wrong with you?" Ryan immediately asked.

"Excuse me?" Was it so obvious her world was about to end? Dani pasted a smile on her face.

"You've been as blue as that sapphire in your ring, there, ever since you came back from your friend's house. I want to know what's upset you."

"I'm really fine—"

"Bull. I don't think you've ever lied to me before. Don't start now."

Dani nearly choked, knowing full well she had lied—well, sort of—about the size of her ranch, and probably without reason since Ryan didn't have designs on her land. Feeling even worse now, she could barely reply. "Okay, okay. I admit it. I am a little down. Barb was very excited, and I remembered what it was like to be so full of hope."

"So the old dreams die hard?"

"Some of them, I guess."

"I knew you felt that way...even if you didn't."

"What are you talking about?"

"Yesterday. I'm talking about yesterday in the truck, when you swore you would never, ever think of getting married again, thanks to that Mick idiot."

"Just because I'm a little bit jealous of Barb doesn't mean that I want a wedding of my own."

"Didn't believe you yesterday afternoon. Don't believe you now."

"For your information, cowboy—"

"I found one! I found one! And it's perfect." Sawyer came on the run, almost slipping on the shiny, checkerboard-patterned floor.

"Whoa there!" Ryan exclaimed as he caught the boy, who immediately handed Dani a radio.

"It matches your kitchen," Sawyer said. "And it plays tapes, too."

"So it does," Dani commented, examining the radio, which would fit perfectly on the windowsill. "An excellent choice, young man. Thank you." Dani slid off the stool and moved toward the checkout, managing two steps before Ryan snatched the radio from her. "Wha—"

"I'm buying it for you."

"You are not!" She tried to take it back.

Ryan just stuck his hand behind his back and shook his head. "Call it a hostess gift. It's the least Sawyer and I can do."

"Yeah," his son agreed with a grin.

After purchase of the radio, which Dani hugged to her chest as if it were worth a million dollars instead of $19.95, the three returned to the police station to pick up Ryan's truck. Sawyer rode back to the ranch with Dani and Ryan followed in his truck.

He watched Dani and Sawyer in the car ahead, noting how they talked and laughed. At one point, Dani swatted at the boy as if he'd said something outrageous—which he probably had—and Ryan grinned, enjoying the sight of their fun. She seemed in better spirits now, he thought, and was glad. He didn't want her to be down about anything, least of all some friend's wedding. A woman as beautiful and kind as Dani would someday find the man she deserved. Ryan never doubted that for a minute.

Without conscious prompting, his mind provided him a fantasy of Dani and some faceless mystery groom, walking down a church aisle somewhere. He imagined how she would look—had looked—in a wedding dress. It was quite a sight, one that took his breath away.

Though he willed his hyperactive brain to shut down or at least change tracks, it rolled on, providing him with other views of Dani's someday nuptials. He saw the groom kiss Dani and remembered how wonderful it was to do that. He watched them dance, and wished he could hold her in his arms again.

And then there was the honeymoon...

With a curse, Ryan turned on the truck radio. He whistled with the country song that blared forth, focusing on each note to shut out a vision of Dani dressed in some sexy nothing and lying in wait for her new husband. He was only half-successful, managing to block nothing more than the groom from his thoughts. Dani remained—sexy, willing, wanting.

Ryan gulped.

It should be me she's waiting for. Me.

They were a match, the two of them, having in common their love of horses, ranching and kids. How sad that fate didn't see it that way.

At least he didn't think fate did.

Ryan's heart began to thump like crazy as he belatedly acknowledged he didn't have a clue what fate had in mind for him. He'd been so focused on his ranch-in-Wyoming dream that he hadn't considered that his Clearwater mugging might've been an act of fate instead of bad luck.

Why, Dani could be his destiny.

Sweet Sadie Sawbucks!

And here he was, ready to pack up and move on, possibly making the biggest mistake of his life. Ryan's stomach knotted at the thought of missing out on the good things that waited—if he made the wrong decision now.

He let his mind dwell on how his life, of late, had seemed to be guided by fate. First, Erica had called from out of the blue. Second, Sawyer had really been his biological kid. Third, a changeover in bosses had made it easy to leave his old job. Fourth, his mugging.

His mugging? An act of the gods?

Possibly, and that meant number five on his list of fateful interventions had to be Dani, coming to his and Sawyer's rescue.

But did he really believe in all that kismet stuff?

Not until now, Ryan admitted, but maybe it was time to open his mind. At any rate, he needed to make future decisions with infinite care and only after a thorough assessment of the people and places around him. Tonight's ranchers' meeting would be a good start, he thought. He'd meet the people in the area, see how he liked them. He'd watch for signs that Colorado, not Wyoming, was where he and his son should live.

As for Dani, well, he'd watch her, as well. Instinct told him that his leaving had as much to do with her blue mood today as any old wedding. Especially since she'd already told him she had no interest in getting married again. Could it be she was falling in love, too? If fate had a hand in things, Ryan realized, there was a damn good chance.

And how did he feel about that?

Ryan just wished he knew.

Dani heard the phone ringing the moment she inserted her house key in the lock of the kitchen door. With a quick twist, she unlocked and opened the door, then snatched up the receiver.

"Hello?"

"Dani, finally. I thought you weren't going to answer, and I really need to talk to you."

"What's up, Jonni? Is tonight's meeting canceled?"

"Oh, no. That's still on. I called because I have some news. Good news."

"What is it?" Dani demanded as Ryan stepped into the kitchen. He said something to Sawyer, distracting Dani from Jonni.

"I'm pregnant."

"What?"

"Pregnant! I'm pregnant!"

Dani squealed her delight. Jonni had been trying for months now and had begun to wonder if it was ever going to happen. "Congratulations!"

"Thanks, honey. We'll celebrate tonight, okay?"

"Okay," Dani agreed, adding, "Will this be a private celebration or are you going to make an announcement?"

"No announcement yet, at least to the general public. You can share my news with Ryan and Sawyer, though. Tell them it's a secret for now."

"Will do," Dani murmured, hanging up moments later. She turned away from the phone to find both of them watching her with obvious curiosity. "It was Jonni." Dani felt herself go suddenly teary and gulped, wondering if her emotion resulted from joy for Jonni, jealousy, or a little of both. "She's, um, pregnant."

"Why, that's great," Ryan murmured.

Though he said the right words, Dani could've sworn his heart wasn't in them. She saw that he was watching her like a hawk and naturally wondered why.

"Do you suppose Ricky wants a little brother or sister?" she asked Sawyer as she moved to put her purse on the kitchen table and slip out of her jacket.

"A brother," Sawyer replied without hesitation as he, too, shook off his jacket and hung it on the hook by the back door.

"He told you?" Dani asked.

"No, but who'd want *two* baby sisters?"

"Good point," Dani said with a laugh. Sawyer headed down the hall, most likely to the bathroom, leaving her alone with Ryan.

"I take it this was planned?" he said.

"Oh, yes. Originally, I think her goal was six kids. Of course, there's been a reality check since then, so number three is probably going to be it."

"Hmm. How many kids do you want, Dani?"

"What?"

"How many kids do you want?" He pulled out a kitchen chair, motioning for her to sit in it. When Dani resisted the idea, Ryan caught her by the shoulders and with a gentle push, demonstrated exactly what he wanted her to do.

She sat. "At one time, I thought I wanted one of each."

"At one time...?" He sat, too.

"I'm twenty-seven years old, Ryan. I'll be lucky if I manage one pregnancy before I'm too old."

"So you envy Jonni."

"Of course I envy her!" Dani snapped and was instantly sorry. It wasn't Ryan's fault she wanted things she couldn't have. At least not directly. Heaven knows she'd relegated all her hopes and dreams to the back closet of her mind before he'd crashed into her life. Now they were out and about again, tripping up her happiness.

Ryan took her hand in both of his, his expression earnest. "It's not too late for you, Dani. Someday the right man will come along, and when he does, you'll make a wonderful wife and mother."

Though tempted to give him a bitter rejoinder, Dani held her tongue. Without a doubt, he spoke those words from the heart. That pleased her.

Not for the first time, she took a good look at him. Not for the first time, she saw a cowboy with sensitivity, who was also responsible, hardworking and, yes, honest. Dani marveled that she'd ever doubted his motives and realized that she had let past troubles blind her to future possibilities. Not that there were any at the moment, at least where Ryan was concerned. And Dani knew there never could be unless she told him the truth about her ranch—an omission that weighed more and more heavily on her mind the better she got to know and love him.

Love.

How easily she thought the word now. How natural it felt.

Yet he stood on the brink of goodbye.

"Dani?"

Abruptly, Dani came to life, easing her hand from Ryan's, managing a smile. "You're right, of course, and I apologize for being such a Gloomy Gus. You won't tell Jonni, will you?"

"Don't be ridiculous."

"Thanks, Ryan. You're a good friend."

"Is that what I am, Dani? Is it?" He sounded so intense she had to wonder what he was thinking.

Dani frowned. "Of course. Don't you think of me that way?"

He hesitated instead of replying, his expression unreadable.

"Ryan?" she questioned, suddenly uncertain. "Do you or do you not consider me a friend?"

His chair scraped against the floor as he stood. Reaching out, he brushed his fingers over her cheek.

"You're a friend all right, Dani," he murmured, bending suddenly to give her a quick, hard kiss. He slipped past, then, and with a thump of heavy boots, headed to the back door, now behind Dani. Stunned, she didn't turn when she heard him open it, but sat, her fingers pressed to lips that still tingled from his kiss. "You're the best damn friend I ever had, and it isn't enough. It's just not enough," she heard him say.

"'Enough'? What do you mean *'enough'*?" she demanded as she twisted around to confront him.

The click of the back door, shutting behind Ryan, was her only reply.

Chapter Nine

Dani never got an answer to her question. A quick peek out the kitchen window revealed that Ryan's long strides had already taken him halfway to the barn. By the time he returned to the house later that evening, Sawyer was underfoot, "helping" her prepare dinner, so she couldn't ask Ryan to explain what he'd said earlier. Surely, she finally decided, if Ryan wanted her to know what he meant by his cryptic comment, he'd tell her. Meanwhile, she guessed she'd have to wonder... and, God help her, hope.

Dani did both, all through a supper strangely quiet. It was as though each of them had secret thoughts or worries they did not want to share. At any rate, little was said except, *Please pass the butter* or *Would you like seconds?*

It was Sawyer who eventually broke the heavy silence. "I just don't understand why we can't stay here."

"But I thought you *wanted* to go to the meeting tonight." Ryan looked bewildered, almost as though he'd been miles away. Dani guessed *Wyoming* and some of her secret, daring hopes crashed against the rocks of reality.

"Not tonight," Sawyer not so patiently replied. "Tomorrow. I'm talking about tomorrow. Why can't we just stay here with Dani instead of moving away? She has plenty of room. We can do all her work and she can cook blueberry pancakes for us every single day." He took a big bite of same—they were having breakfast for supper tonight—demonstrating how delectable he considered them.

With an apologetic glance at Dani, who actually thought the idea a wonderful one, Ryan quickly shook his head. "Living with Dani was okay in an emergency, son, but it's not a long-term option."

"What's 'longtime option'?" Sawyer asked.

"Term. Long-*term* option. It means, well, a permanent choice." Ryan passed his son a napkin and nodded for him to clean up the spill of syrup trailing down his chin. "In other words, our staying here is something we can't do forever."

Sawyer dutifully wiped his face, then took a drink of milk, which left him a chalky white mustache. "Why not?" he asked, setting down his glass.

"Because traditionally, er, *usually*, men and women who aren't related or married don't live in the same house."

"Then get married," Sawyer suggested with solid, eight-year-old logic and utter seriousness.

Dani waited with interest for Ryan's reply, but in vain. Since the cat she didn't own seemed to have stolen his tongue, she felt obliged to take over the argument to end what had become an awkward silence.

"A man and woman should be in love when they get married." She looked pointedly at Ryan, hoping he would jump right in and say that he loved her so she could admit that she loved him, too. He didn't, of course.

"*I* love you," his son said, instead, words that nearly knocked Dani out of her chair. They couldn't have come easy for him, this child who, mere days ago, had barely tolerated hugs. "Do you love me back?"

"Of course I do," Dani replied, words from the heart.

"Then will you marry *me?*"

Tears sprang to Dani's eyes—tears she blinked back. "I'm very flattered you'd ask, but I'm afraid you're not old enough to get a marriage license."

Sawyer gaped at her. "You mean, you have to have a *license?*"

"Yes, you do."

"Like the one on your car?"

Dani bit back a smile. "This one is made out of paper. You keep it in a safe place."

"Oh. How much does it cost?"

"I'm not sure, actually. I just know that you have to be eighteen to get it." She did not add that sixteen was the magic number if one had parental consent.

Sawyer sighed as though the weight of the world lay on his small shoulders. Dani's heart ached for this precious child, so earnest in his proposal, and for the innocence of youth, when every problem had a black or white solution.

"But what am I going to do without you?" Sawyer whispered as his bottom lip began to tremble and his dark eyes to glimmer with unshed tears.

Impulsively, Dani slipped from her chair and dropped to her knees beside him. Sawyer threw his arms around her neck, and Dani hugged him back with abandon.

"You'll miss me sometimes, like I'll miss you, but before long you'll be just fine," she promised him, her words a mere whisper against his ear. She wished she could say the same for herself, but knew better.

She was no resilient child, waking up to a world of high adventure every day. She was a grown woman, who didn't know what she would do without Sawyer's childish witticisms and laughter, Ryan's stolen kisses. In a few short days, her life had been turned upside down forever, but not for the better... at least not if they left tomorrow as planned. And while in the past Dani had made successful adjustments to loneliness and boredom, this time she did not believe she could do it.

Dani's gaze met Ryan's across the table once again. He looked stricken. They exchanged a glance—long and speculative. But he still said nothing, nothing at all. Feeling suddenly desperate, Dani heard herself blurt out an offer to remodel the bunkhouse for him and Sawyer if they would agree to stay.

"It isn't *that* bad," she concluded. "Nothing an exterminator, a painter and a plumber couldn't put to rights. You two could have a say in the redecorating, of course, and fix it up exactly the way you wanted."

Sawyer, face bright with new hope, looked from Dani to his dad. "Did ya hear that, Dad? If we stayed here with Dani, we wouldn't have to build a house. You said that's the part you hated most about moving to Wyoming, remember?"

Ryan did remember, but that had nothing to do with the issue at hand. "Dani's offer is very generous," he told Sawyer. "We still can't do it, though."

"But why not?" Sawyer asked once again, his tone as petulant as the set of his jaw was stubborn.

Why not? Ryan could think of several reasons, not the least of which was that he didn't have the nerve to do what his son had just done—tell Dani he loved her, then propose.

And why did he, a thirty-three-year-old rancher who spoke perfectly good English have such a problem verbalizing his emotion, his desire? Because he'd never felt this way before and therefore had a million insecurities to deal with. What if Dani broke his heart? What if he broke hers? In his experience, that's what happened when a man and woman bared their souls to one another. And those tragedies were just the worst of it. There were myriad tortures of lesser degrees to be endured until that fateful finale, tortures from which he—and Dani—still bore scars.

Suddenly depressed, Ryan silently considered all the options open to him at that moment. The first, going to Wyoming as planned, held little appeal now. Ryan guessed Dani could be blamed for that. The second, accepting her generous job offer and staying in Colorado, held even less, probably because it meant abandoning a lifelong dream to be self-employed.

"Dad?"

The third, telling Dani that he loved her and proposing—clearly Sawyer's choice—held the least appeal of all, and for the same reason, Ryan realized, as the second option. Should Dani accept his proposal, she would undoubtedly want him to live with her *on her ranch,* which had, after all, been in her family for years and years.

"Hey, Dad."

Though marriage traditionally meant sharing, Ryan would always know that the ranch was Dani's and Dani's alone. In other words, there would be no difference between being the husband of a landowner and being the foreman to one. He'd still work for someone else on a ranch that was not his. True, the fringe benefits would be heaven on earth, but—

"Dad!"

With a start, Ryan realized that both Dani and Sawyer were staring at him expectantly, as if waiting for an answer. Unfortunately, he'd forgotten the question.

"What?" he asked sheepishly.

"Why...not?" Clearly, Sawyer thought his dad had gone 'round the bend, as perhaps he had.

"Why not what?"

"Da-ad," Sawyer groaned.

"Okay, okay." Guessing the question, Ryan searched for an answer his son could easily comprehend. "We can't stay here because I want a place of my own. I've been a nobody too long. I need to be my own boss."

"But—"

"But nothing. It's time, son. If I don't take steps now, I might be a hired hand forever."

Ryan felt Dani's heavy stare and risked a glance at her. She looked thoughtful, as though she sensed his complicated thought process and knew he wasn't telling all. Did she realize her ranch had come between them? he wondered.

Sawyer argued no more, whether because he sensed his dad wasn't in the mood or because he actually understood the unspoken, Ryan didn't know. It was enough that he didn't have to explain further the reason they had no choice but to move on as planned.

Ryan kept the conversation on other things all the way to Jonni's that night. Since Dani knew the way—and his truck had a gypsy look about it—she drove her car, pointing out the ranches en route, telling Ryan a bit about each of their owners so he'd be a little familiar with the people he was going to meet.

In a way, Ryan dreaded the meeting, which drew a crowd of around thirty or so men, women and children. He didn't really belong, after all, and had no stake in the outcome. Besides, he didn't know a soul except Dani and Jonni...or so he thought. As it turned out, he ran into not one, but two cowboys, now area ranchers, whom he'd known ten years ago when traveling the rodeo circuit: Sam Dwyer and Billy Mason.

During the premeeting chitchat that took place in Jonni's spacious dining room, living room and kitchen, the three men talked over old times. Ryan kept details of his current affairs to a minimum, saying little more than that he'd just completed a run of bad luck and was about to change it by moving on. Upon hearing his plans, both old friends urged Ryan to put down roots in Colorado instead of Wyoming, an idea that actually began to evolve into a viable option four as the men talked on.

"Not that Wyoming isn't pretty," Sam said. "It's something else, for sure. Colorado just can't be topped to my way of thinking." Small and wiry, Sam had been a hell of a bull rider in his heyday and, as a result, competed all over the United States and the world. Ryan respected both his talent as a rancher and his opinion as a traveler.

"I'm wanting at least six hundred or more acres for starters," Ryan said.

"There's land to be had, I expect," Billy told him. In contrast to Sam, Billy stood well over six feet tall and had the physique of a flagpole. "Don't know how much, myself, and don't know for sure where. I suggest you keep your eyes and ears open tonight. If no one here has any they'll let go of, there's a good chance you'll hear about someone who does. Sam and me'll spread the word for you, won't we, Sam?" His friend nodded. "I'll tell Sheila, too."

"Sheila?"

"My wife. She's around here somewhere and there's no woman better at hearing the latest."

"You're *married?*"

Billy grinned. "Four years now. I've got two boys, too. Twins."

So the last of the bronc-bustin' bachelors had finally settled down. Ryan couldn't believe it. He turned to Sam. "What about you? Surely *you* never found a saint willing to tackle a reform."

Sam grinned and pointed to a vivacious redhead standing across the room with a group of women. "Bet you didn't know angels had hair that color."

Ryan shook his head. "I thought they were all blondes," he murmured with a covert glance at Dani, standing near Sawyer, Ricky and Jonni at the kitchen door. "Kids?"

Sam held up three fingers.

Ryan just shook his head and murmured, "Damn."

Sam shrugged sheepishly. "What about you? Heard any wedding bells in the last ten years?"

"Nope. I've got a son, though. Over there by Dani Sellica."

Just as the men's gazes found Sawyer, Dani began to tussle with the boy, both of them laughing like crazy. Ryan's heart turned a backflip at the sight. Sam and Billy grinned.

"Looks like he's in good hands," Billy commented, running one of his own hands through blond hair cut slightly shaggy and slicked straight back. Always a bit of a character, he sported a handlebar mustache. Ryan wondered if his wife let him work as a rodeo clown, something "Billy Boy" had done for years, and done well.

"Yeah," Ryan said. "We've, uh, been staying at her place, doing some work for her."

"No kidding?" Billy sounded inordinately surprised.

"Just since Christmas," Ryan quickly supplied, aware of the way one of them elbowed the other. Now, what did that mean? "Something wrong?"

Billy shrugged and gave his mustache a twirl. "Dani could sure use the help, I guess, alone with a place that size. I just thought after all that business with Mick—" He broke off abruptly, as if unsure he should be sharing her personal business with someone who was, to her, a virtual stranger.

"I know about Mick."

That earned Ryan a speculative stare from both men. Suddenly he wished he hadn't been so blunt. "Dani was explaining why she doesn't want to hire anyone on a permanent basis...not that I intend to work for someone else ever again. I don't. We were just, uh, clarifying some things."

Dead silence followed his stumbling, unnecessary explanation.

"Your boy seems to like her a lot." This from Sam, who once again watched Dani and Sawyer.

A quick glance his son's way revealed that the boy was still standing beside Dani. Ryan wondered if Sawyer felt the imminence of tomorrow's departure as much as he did.

"She's been good to us. Real good. We'll miss her." That last just slipped out—a confession he wanted to take back as soon as he heard the echo of it.

"All the more reason to hang around," Sam said, slapping Ryan heartily on the back.

At that moment, Jonni walked up to them. "Ryan, would you mind letting loose with that whistle of yours to get everyone's attention?" She grinned at Sam and Billy. "You've never heard anything like it."

Both men, who undoubtedly claimed the same talent, which came in handy working cattle on the plains, just laughed. Ryan obediently whistled. The room went abruptly silent.

"If we're going to get anything done," Jonni said, raising her voice so that it could be heard by all, "we'd better get started. I've set up some chairs in the living room, though admittedly not enough, thanks to this great turnout. But hopefully, everyone will be able to get where they can see and hear okay."

What followed was a shuffling of bodies that resulted in the females being seated, and the males, in the cowboy way, holding up the walls. Ryan stole a moment to let his gaze wander the roomful of strangers, noting that he felt oddly at home, almost as if he belonged.

A trick of decorating? he wondered, eyeing the ruffled curtains, braided rugs and family photos that made the room so homey. Or was it the people?

Ryan looked to his left and right and realized he didn't know the men on either side of him, so was surprised when one of them asked, sotto voce, if he and Dani were "seeing each other."

"We're friends," Ryan told him, his voice just as low.

Not two seconds after, he was asked the question again, this time by the man on his other side and in a slightly different manner.

"Are you going out with Dani Sellica?"

"No," Ryan replied. Dismayed that he might've put Dani in an awkward position, Ryan located her, seated on a folding chair across the room. She and the woman sitting next to her had their heads together, as if in private conversation. The woman glanced rather pointedly at Ryan, then asked Dani something. Ryan saw Dani shake her head, before she, too, looked over at him.

Noting that she appeared a bit flustered, Ryan guessed that she was having to field questions about them, too. He almost wished they'd prepared an answer in advance so their stories would be the same. One slip of the tongue would be a major disaster, he thought—at least for Dani. He, himself, wouldn't be around to experience any aftershocks.

The meeting moved right along, probably because Jonni, a woman with a cause, led it. Her husband, a big man named Ben, said little, but his presence behind the scenes spoke volumes for his support of her campaign. An hour after Jonni's call to order, she announced a ten-minute break, clearly pleased with what had been accomplished. Though she urged everyone to partake of the snacks that had miraculously appeared on the dining table, Ryan stepped outside with Sam, who claimed he needed some fresh air.

What Sam really needed was a smoke, as did a few other of their neighbors, one of whom introduced himself to Ryan as Duke Littlejohn. Ryan noticed that when Littlejohn joined them, Sam left to take care of forgotten business indoors. An excuse? Ryan naturally wondered, suddenly wary.

"I noticed you came tonight with Dani Sellica," Littlejohn commented, his face almost obscured by a cloud of pungent cigar smoke. "You two an item?"

"I've been helping her out some around her place, is all," Ryan replied, trying not to take offense. Dani was one classy lady who'd had more than her share of bad luck. And since as a rule cowboys were rather territorial, most any of them would naturally be protective of their own and, therefore, curious about Ryan, an outsider.

"Good." Littlejohn puffed again on the cigar. "She doesn't have any business running that ranch alone."

Ryan, who couldn't imagine why not, noted that Littlejohn looked to be in his late sixties—a handsome man with steel gray eyes and snow-white hair. He wore jeans, dark blue and sharply creased, snakeskin boots and belt, western-style shirt, leather vest and a Stetson. A bit of a dandy, Ryan surmised for no other reason than gut instinct, which explained why Sam, redneck to the bone, wouldn't like him.

"Actually, I'm leaving for Wyoming tomorrow," Ryan said.

"That so? I could've sworn I overheard someone say you're looking for some land in these parts."

He'd heard that already? Apparently, the cowboy grapevine worked as efficiently in Colorado as it did in Oklahoma. "Half looking is more like it." Ryan knocked some dried mud off the toe of his boot and tried not to inhale too deeply of air that was no longer "fresh," thanks to the smelly cigar. "Know of any?"

"As a matter of fact, I have one thousand acres I'd sell to the right cowboy."

Ryan, who didn't believe in good luck—at least his own—or coincidence, frowned, immediately a little suspicious. "Where's it located?"

"Just east of Dani's place. A fence is all that separates what's mine from what's hers."

"Yeah?" Odd that neither Sam nor Billy had mentioned it. "Been on the market long?"

"It's not on the market now, at least I haven't advertised it, if that's what you're asking. But I have been thinking about selling, and something tells me you might be the buyer I've been waiting for."

Ryan didn't know what to say. Part of him wanted to jump on the offer. The other part considered it a little too pat, too perfect.

Kind of like Dani's needing—but not needing—a hired hand just when he needed a job and a place to stay.

"You're planning on running cattle, I guess." A smoke ring rose into the dark of the winter night.

Ryan nodded.

"My place would be perfect for it."

"If it's so perfect, why are you selling?"

Littlejohn laughed, clearly amused by Ryan's sharp question. "I have more land besides that, which I'm not going to sell, plus a thirty-five-hundred acre spread in Texas that I'm going to build on come spring."

Ryan whistled low to show how impressed he was. "Then how come you haven't offered this land to some of the other ranchers around here before now? They have more right to it than me, and I'm thinking there are some who might jump at the chance to expand their holdings."

"I told you, I've been waiting for the right cowboy. Besides, I'm not very popular among these folks, thanks to some past misunderstandings. I'm not sure they'd buy from me. I'm damn sure I don't want to sell to them."

Ryan, who suddenly realized that everyone else had gone back inside to the meeting, wasn't surprised to hear that. Sam had sure made tracks the moment Littlejohn joined them.

"What kind of misunderstandings?" He had no intention of buying property resulting from crooked dealings or, God forbid, foreclosure on some poor cowpoke who couldn't make his note.

"The land is mine fair and square, if that's what you're asking," Littlejohn replied, an answer that wasn't exactly reassuring. He then quoted a price per acre that sounded reasonable, which, oddly enough, only made Ryan more suspicious.

"I'll need to think about it."

"Of course." Littlejohn reached back for his wallet and from it extracted a business card, which he handed to Ryan. "Take your time. Go on up to Wyoming and see what you can find there. Then give me a call either way, will you?"

"I guess I could do that."

"Good." Littlejohn flipped the remains of his cigar into the yard, where it sizzled briefly in the snow. "I'd appreciate it if you'd keep this offer under your hat, Mr. Given."

"Ryan."

"Ryan, then. I have a certain amount of...well...power in this area. I'm not ready to relinquish it just yet by announcing my moving plans."

"All right," Ryan murmured somewhat uneasily as Littlejohn nodded a brisk goodbye and vanished inside. Alone on the front porch, he could barely assimilate all that had happened.

After the meeting ended, Dani handed Ryan the car keys, claiming she had a terrible headache. He obliged by driving, and since neither Dani nor Sawyer said a word all the way home, had plenty of opportunity to think about the timing of Littlejohn's offer.

Fate again? he had to wonder.

From all appearances, Duke Littlejohn sure seemed to be the perfect solution to Ryan's problems, right when he needed one most. That, more than location, size or price of the land made Ryan cautious. And he finally had to admit that no matter how wonderful the land offer seemed, something about it didn't feel right.

He decided he'd stop in Clearwater on the way out of the state tomorrow and talk to Cliff Meeks, who was in a position to know everything about everybody. If the land turned out to be all right, maybe he and Sawyer wouldn't be leaving Colorado, after all. Maybe he'd just head back to Dani's and propose to her, knowing that if she accepted, he would go into the marriage with land—*adjoining* land, to boot—of his own.

Upon arrival at the ranch at around eleven o'clock, Sawyer, who'd bathed before the meeting, headed straight to bed. Dani, however, went only as far as the kitchen, where she shed her jacket, then searched her "medicine shelf" in the pantry for a headache remedy.

"Where does it hurt?" Ryan hovered at her elbow.

"Here." Dani laid a hand on her brow line.

"Tension, I'll bet."

The look she gave him said, *Of course, you big dummy!* though she said not a word. After Dani swallowed a couple of aspirin, she started for the hall door, an exit Ryan halted by grabbing her arm.

"Sit down for a minute," he said as he pulled out one of the kitchen chairs from the table. "If your headache is really a tension headache, I think I can help."

"I'd rather wait on the aspirin—"

"Sit, Dani. I know what I'm doing," Ryan said and then almost laughed. If ever a man *didn't* know what he was doing—at least about everything else—it was Ryan Given.

With obvious reluctance, Dani perched on the edge of the chair. Firmly, but gently, Ryan urged her back in the seat by grasping her shoulders in his hands and tugging. She did as requested, but remained ramrod straight, her body tense, her muscles unyielding.

"Relax, for Pete's sake," Ryan blurted out as he kneaded her shoulders, back and neck with his fingers.

Dani resisted at first, but then accepted his gentle ministrations in stages, beginning with a soft "Oh my..." of defeat. When she reached the point of being so relaxed that Ryan's probing fingers met no resistance, making the massage difficult, he slipped his left arm around her body, just above her breasts, and caught hold of her right shoulder with his hand to brace her.

With a sigh, she rested her cheek on his biceps. Ryan's temperature shot up several degrees and his heart began to hammer. Afraid Dani might notice—his chest was pressed against her left shoulder—he tried to pull back. At once she grabbed his forearm, preventing the move.

Puzzled, hopeful, Ryan stood in indecision for what seemed an eternity before he felt the coolness of something wet on his sleeve. A tear, he realized, heart sinking, even as another fell and soaked the cotton fabric.

Overcome with love, Ryan could not resist putting his arm around her in a hug from behind that included the back of the chair. He buried his face in her hair, breathing in the scent that was so distinctly Dani. Ryan suspected the fragrance would haunt his dreams for a long, long time, maybe forever.

He trailed his lips over her hair then down the side of her face, planting a kiss on her temple, her earlobe, her neck. For a second, she did not respond beyond a slight tightening of the hold she had on his arm. Then she caught one of his hands in hers and raised it to her lips so she could kiss the back of it. Encouraged, Ryan shifted his stance and dropped to his knees in front of her chair, their bodies touching. Dani raised her head of necessity as he did so. Their gazes locked.

He noted that her eyes swam with tears still unshed.

"Dani, I—" Just in time, he caught himself. He what? Loved her? Was he really going to propose to this woman he barely knew, without any idea where they could go from there?

What a fool he was. What a damn fool. Hadn't he learned the hard way never to act without thought to the consequences? Wasn't his son living proof of what could happen if a man shucked responsibility and followed impulse? In truth, Sawyer's very existence could be blamed on the passion of a moment, and Ryan's lack of planning had resulted in the mishandling of his own and his boy's affairs. He owed it to Sawyer—to himself—to do better this time around.

"Just say what's in your heart, Ryan. Please."

Ryan read the hope on Dani's face—suddenly knew without a doubt she would welcome a declaration of love and give him one in return. God, but he wanted to take the leap, to hear those magic words, to throw caution to the winter wind. But would that really solve all his problems, or just create new ones?

"Dani, I...I mean *I'm*, uh, really going to miss you," he stammered, his gaze now focused on the wall. "Sawyer and I both are. You took us into your home. You made Christmas extra special for him and helped me through some rough spots. We owe you. I intend to repay you as soon as I can. And I want you to know that if you ever need anything... anything at all... all you've got to do is yell, and I'll come running."

"All the way from Wyoming?" Her words were as cold as a bucket of Colorado snow dumped over his head. A chill raced down his spine.

"Absolutely."

"Well, thanks a million, cowboy," she said, her eyes suddenly glittering with something besides tears. "But even if I could yell that loud, I doubt I'd bother. You obviously don't have anything I need."

With a look he could not decipher, Dani tore free of his embrace, leaped to her feet and dashed down the hall. Ryan heard the slam of her door and an ominous metallic click. He winced at the sound, knowing that thanks to the cowardly goodbye speech of his, she'd just locked him out of more than her bedroom.

She'd locked him out of her heart.

Chapter Ten

A barrage of wonderful smells greeted Ryan when he walked into the kitchen early Tuesday morning. Surprised to find Dani already up and at 'em, he eyed with amazement the picnic basket sitting on the table, brimming with all manner of edibles.

"What's this?" he asked, dispensing with the usual *good morning*.

"I'm packing a lunch and some snacks for you guys," Dani replied without so much as a glance his way. "I've also baked that cake I promised Sawyer. It should be cool enough to frost by the time we finish breakfast." She took a rectangular pan rounded up with a dark chocolate cake out of the oven and set it on a wooden rack on the counter. Turning to face him, she pulled a pair of colorful oven mitts from her hands. "I know you're anxious to get to Wyoming. This is the least I can do to speed you on your way."

One look at the dark circles under her eyes revealed she'd slept as little as Ryan had. A wave of guilt washed over him.

"Dani, I'm sorry—"

"For what?" she interjected sharply. "Having a life? Well, contrary to appearances, I have one, too. So there's no need for you to feel guilty about getting on with yours."

Stung by the rejoinder, Ryan didn't trust himself to speak. Abruptly, he spun on his heel, and muttering some lame excuse about waking Sawyer, headed down the hall. He found his son lost in sweet dreams and reluctantly woke him to reality before returning to the kitchen. The second he walked back into the sunny, fragrant room that was the heart of the house, Dani stepped close.

"I'm sorry I snapped at you," she said, reaching out to lay a hand on his shoulder. "I'm a little stressed about this goodbye. I know it's going to be tough for Sawyer, and I don't want him upset."

So it was Sawyer she was worried about, not his dad. That was as it should be and it definitely should not have hurt, he told himself, but it did.

"Yeah. I hate it, too," Ryan murmured awkwardly. "He really wants to stay and he doesn't understand why it's just not possible."

Dani, who clearly had something on her mind, hesitated for a heartbeat before blurting out, "If I promised to keep my distance—if I swore that things between us would be strictly business from now on—would you reconsider staying and working for me?"

Ryan's jaw dropped. She thought *she* was the reason he was leaving? God, didn't anyone understand him? "Dani, I—"

"Never mind," she suddenly interjected, cutting off his halting attempt to set her straight. "That was stupid of me." Spinning away, she returned to the stove to stir a pan of oatmeal that didn't appear to need her attention.

Ryan followed. Grasping Dani's shoulders, he turned her to face him, then took the spoon from her hand and set it aside.

"When I leave today, it will not be because of you but in spite of you," he told her. *"Understand?"* He gave her a little shake.

Dani's gaze searched his face for what seemed an eternity. Then she sighed. "Actually, I don't. I thought you were happy here."

"My boy and I have both been happy here," Ryan said. "That's what makes leaving the hardest thing I've ever had to do."

"Then why do it?" Dani demanded, eyes glistening with moisture. She gripped his biceps as though to keep him there forever.

Ryan's heart twisted. "Because I have nothing to offer you, Dani. *Nothing at all*—beyond sound cowboy logic and a body that's seen better days."

"But that's exactly—" she began, words his lips stole from hers. Ryan kissed Dani long and hard and with the urgency of unsatisfied passion, the finality of a last good-bye. When he raised his head again, he held her close for a moment, his chin resting on the top of her head. Dani clung to him, her breath ragged, her heart pounding so fiercely he felt the vibration. How easy it would be to settle for this, he realized.

And how long before he regretted it?

"I have to be your equal," he said more to himself than to Dani, who tipped her head back and frowned up at him.

"What are you guys doing?"

At the sound of Sawyer's voice so close by, Dani flinched and tried to pull free. Ryan found he could not let her go.

"Group hug," he replied. "And what's missing is you!" Ryan held his arm out to the boy. Taking his cue, Dani did the same. At once Sawyer hurled himself at the two of them. They engulfed him into their circle of love.

Love?

Oh, yeah. So intense, so powerful it lit up the kitchen.

But was it the right kind—the forever kind? he wondered. Or just that of friends? And what about the times they'd come so close to intimacy? Where did that fall into the scheme of things? Suddenly afraid of an answer that might tempt him to compromise his lifelong dreams, Ryan abruptly released Dani and Sawyer.

"Look what Dani's done," he murmured, his voice unsteady. He pointed to the picnic basket, which Sawyer eyed with little enthusiasm and less curiosity. "She's even baked that chocolate cake."

When Sawyer still said nothing, Ryan glanced away, only to intercept Dani's heavy, questioning gaze. Clearly, she waited for Ryan to speak, to announce a change in plans or at least a delay until they could talk further. He just shook his head.

Sawyer looked from the picnic basket to Dani to his dad. Ryan, who could tell his son sensed the undercurrents of emotion, half expected the boy to raise questions or argue. But Sawyer did neither.

They sat down to a breakfast of oatmeal, though no one seemed to have much appetite. When they were finished, the males helped Dani clear the table one last time, then moved to their respective rooms to pack while she frosted the cake, as promised.

The clock in the living room chimed the hour—eight o'clock—just as Ryan stepped back into the kitchen, suitcase in hand. He couldn't bear to look at Dani, so he averted his gaze. She seemed to be doing the same. At any rate, she gave all her attention to Sawyer, who saw the chocolate cake, now frosted and waiting, and burst into tears.

Parting proved difficult for everyone. Ryan focused on the task at hand, almost brusque in his efforts to hide his tumultuous emotions as he tossed their belongings into the back of his pickup. Dani hugged Ryan only briefly, but held Sawyer for a long, long time, soothing the distraught child with promises of phone calls, letters and even visits, and some other things Ryan couldn't hear. She and Sawyer then made one last trip to the barn to say goodbye to the boy's calf, which would stay with Dani until weaned.

By the time Ryan sat behind the steering wheel in the cab of his truck, the chocolate cake container on the seat between him and Sawyer, he felt emotionally wrung-out, oddly flat. Never once did he mention Duke Littlejohn or a possible land purchase. Why do that until he knew the facts—until he made some sort of decision?

"So you're really leaving." Cliff Meeks muttered the words with a shake of his head that said he couldn't quite believe it.

"This isn't a big-screen western where the cowboy and the lady ride off into the sunset together," Ryan reminded him with a sardonic smile. They sat together in the police chief's office, while Sawyer bought soft drinks from the vending machine in the break room down the hall.

Cliff laughed softly. "I guess you're right, but I swear I had a feeling about you two."

Ryan shrugged that off. "I didn't come by this morning just to say goodbye. I need some information, and I think you're the man in the know."

Cliff lifted an eyebrow. "Try me."

"I'm wanting the scoop on a rancher named Littlejohn."

"You mean Duke Littlejohn? Dani's stepfather?"

Ryan's jaw dropped. "Duke Littlejohn is Dani's stepfather, the one who stole her land?" He couldn't believe it.

His comment seemed to take Cliff aback. "Actually, the courts awarded him one-half of Eileen Sellica's estate—that's Dani's mother—when she died. He got one thousand acres in all."

The same one thousand acres he was trying to sell? Ryan wondered. He glanced absently at Sawyer, who'd just entered the office with three canned soft drinks. "So he came by it fair and square?" Ryan took one of the proffered cans.

"Well, square, anyway. I have my own opinion about the fair part, as does most everybody else around here. We never really thought he was entitled to half of the Sellica land. He sure as hell didn't need the property, which had been in Dani's family for years." Cliff accepted the soft drink Sawyer thrust at him, then watched as the boy headed back to the lounge and the television blaring there. "I think a 75-25 split would've been more equitable. Dani, of course, doesn't think he should've gotten anything, but then she never liked him." Cliff studied Ryan for a moment. "May *I* ask why *you're* asking?"

"Littlejohn's offered to sell me a thousand acres. Probably the Sellica land. He did mention it butts up against Dani's place."

"On the east?"

Ryan nodded.

"That'd be it." Cliff looked thoughtful. "Wonder what he's up to now...?"

"Said that he wasn't getting rid of all his property, just that thousand acres. Said that he didn't want to sell to anyone around here. That he's been waiting for the 'right cowboy.'" With a shrug, Ryan popped the top of his drink. "That's me, according to him." Cliff did the same, and the men sat in silence for a moment, sipping and second-guessing Duke Littlejohn's motives. "You'd think he'd offer it to Dani, first, wouldn't you?"

Cliff shook his head. "Not likely. They've been feuding for years. As for one of the other ranchers around here...let me just say that there's been no love lost between Littlejohn and his neighbors ever since he and Mick tried to swindle Dani out of her timber rights."

"I gathered that, but selling the land to her—or to anyone else, for that matter—would still make more sense than selling to a stranger. We couldn't have talked more than a minute at the meeting last night before he made the offer."

"So you two met at the road meeting, huh?" Cliff mulled that over. "Anyone ask if you and Dani were involved?"

Ryan winced. "Too many to count."

"And what'd you tell them?"

"That I was just the hired help, of course."

"Then there's your reason. Duke undoubtedly heard that and offered you the land to spite Dani and everyone else."

"So if I buy the place and sell it back to her, I'll be righting an old wrong." Ryan liked the idea of doing that even though it as good as eliminated—or at the least delayed—his chances of buying a ranch in the area.

"And besting Littlejohn at his own game, I might add, though what Dani's gonna do with two thousand acres is beyond me."

Two thousand acres? Only then did Ryan realize the full implications of the past five minutes' conversation. If Duke Littlejohn had inherited one thousand acres from his wife in a fifty-fifty split, then that meant Dani owned one thousand acres, too.

But she'd said she only owned two hundred.

Hadn't she...?

Thinking back, Ryan realized she had never really shared the total size of her acreage and then remembered his feeling that it was a deliberate omission. Apparently he'd been right, he now thought grimly. And though Ryan could guess why she'd kept the whole truth from him—who had better reason to mistrust a cowboy in search of a home?—the deception angered and hurt.

Clearly, he was light-years ahead of her emotionally, which meant he was on the money about what he'd felt in the kitchen that morning. If it was love at all, it was not the right kind. People in love did not keep secrets from each other.

"What are you going to do about the offer?" Cliff's question barely penetrated Ryan's haze of confusion and indecision.

"Nothing just yet. I owe it to myself to check out Wyoming, as planned." The answer came automatically from Ryan's subconscious and the moment he heard its echo, he knew it was the only one. He did owe himself a trip to Wyoming. As for Dani, absence would either make his—and her—heart grow fonder, as the old saying promised, or it'd be out of sight, out of mind. Time away would tell, he guessed, coming to an abrupt decision to hit the road, and the sooner the better. Undoubtedly, distance would put the whole thing in perspective.

Or was that just a handy excuse to stay ignorant of the truth for a while longer?

Pushing such thoughts to a far corner of his mind, Ryan extended his hand to Cliff and smiled. "Thanks for all you've done for me and my boy, Chief Meeks."

Cliff, who now stood, shook Ryan's hand, then covered it with his own instead of releasing it. "Just glad I could help, son."

Oddly moved by Cliff's use of the word *son*—a southernism that signified affection—Ryan nodded, got his hand back and headed to the lounge, where Sawyer sat on the couch, his gaze glued to the television.

"Hey, Dad!" the boy exclaimed the moment Ryan joined him. "Lookit this." He motioned his dad further into the room, then pointed to the TV, the screen of which was filled with an image of a sparkling diamond engagement ring. Ryan took in the sight and realized his son was watching a home-shopping show. "They've only got twenty-five left at this low, low price. You'd better call quick."

Ryan blinked in surprise. "Now, what do I need a diamond ring for?"

"To give to Dani," Sawyer replied, the next second leaping off the couch and throwing his arms around his startled dad's waist. "Don't ya want to go back and marry her, Dad?" he demanded, tipping his head back to look dear ol' dad in the eye. "Don't ya?"

Ryan sighed and smoothed his son's dark hair, then gave him a kiss on the top of his head. "Have you already forgotten what we talked about yesterday—about how two people should love one another before they get married?"

"You mean, you don't love her?" Sawyer looked incredulous—as if doubting that anyone could not love his precious Dani.

"*I* love *her,* yeah, but I'm afraid she doesn't love me back."

"Sure she does."

"How do you know?"

"Because she told me so, that's how."

Ryan tensed and let his son go. "What?"

Sawyer nodded eager affirmation. "She told me so."

"When?"

"This morning. Didn't you hear her?"

Ryan shook his head as he frantically tried to recall anything Dani might've said to make Sawyer think she was in love. "When, exactly, did she tell you this?"

"Right before we left. We were standing by the truck. She promised to come for a visit. She said she loved us both."

Oh. Ryan let out his pent-up breath in a slow hiss of regret since *that* hardly counted. "She didn't really mean it," he said. "Now, it's nine-thirty. We've got to go."

"But Dad—"

"No argument. *We've got to go.*"

Sawyer's shoulders slumped with defeat, but he didn't persist. Together, the two of them left the police station, walked to the parking lot and got into the truck.

Ryan inserted the key into the lock and gave it a twist. When the engine roared to life, he reversed the vehicle out of its spot, then drove to the exit, where he sat waiting for a break in the traffic. Out of the corner of his eye, he noticed that his son stared at him intently.

"What is it?" Ryan asked, turning his full attention to Sawyer, who looked ready to burst into tears.

"I'm worried about Dani."

"You're forgetting that she has lived alone on that ranch for years and is perfectly capable of taking care of it and herself."

"I know *that.*" Clearly, the boy had little patience with his thick-headed parent.

"Then why are you worried about her?" Ryan nonetheless asked.

"'Cause she's a liar, and Granny Wright told me what happens to *them.*"

Ryan blinked in surprise. "Dani's no liar."

"But you just told me—"

"No such thing."

"You said she didn't mean it when she said she loved us both. Doesn't that make her a liar?"

Ryan could only stare at his deductive son and wonder how to answer. "Dani's no liar," he finally repeated somewhat lamely, knowing in his heart of hearts he spoke the truth.

"So she does love us both?"

"If she says so, yes. But—" Ryan held up both hands to ward off the then-why-not-marry-her argument he knew would follow "—there's love, and there's love."

"What?" The boy looked puzzled . . . and no wonder.

Ryan sighed, checked to be sure there wasn't another vehicle waiting for him to exit the parking lot, then tried again. "Love means a lot of different things."

"I still don't get it."

"Okay, okay . . . give me a minute. Surely I can explain this." He thought hard, then snapped his fingers in sudden inspiration. "You love your calf, don't you?"

"Sure."

"And your calf loves you?"

"Uh-huh."

"So are you two going to get married?"

Sawyer giggled. "That's silly. Guys don't marry calves."

"Of course not. I'm just trying to explain that there are different kinds of love, and a man and woman have to love each other in the same special way before they can get married."

Sawyer frowned, justifiably baffled. "Do you mean that Dani loves you like a pet calf and not like a husband?"

Ryan nearly swallowed his tongue. "No. Yes. Well, sort of. Dani loves me as a, um, friend. Yeah, a friend. Not as a boyfriend or husband."

Sawyer's eyes lit up. "Ohhh. Like I love Heidi Mimms?" He named one of his favorite Arkansas playmates.

"Exactly." Ryan sagged with relief.

"Well, why didn't you just say so?" Sawyer asked, crossing his arms over his chest and giving his dad a good-grief! look.

The hoot of a horn brought Ryan to life. With a glance in his rearview mirror and a wave of apology, he eased onto the street and managed to make it to the very next intersection before Sawyer screamed, "Stop!"

Instantly, Ryan hit the brake and looked all around for the unsuspecting pedestrian he was surely about to mow down. He saw no one.

"What is it, son?"

"We forgot to take Dani's picture." The boy looked absolutely stricken and ready to cry again.

Well, hell. Rapidly, Ryan considered his options and realized there could be only one if he wanted any peace in his life—return to Dani's. And since he was now going to go there, why not confront her about concealing the size of her ranch? That rankled. God, how it rankled. He had to know if she honestly believed him capable of stealing her land. If so, then maybe what they'd shared wasn't love of any degree, but pure lust. His lips pursed with determination, Ryan looked ahead and spied a convenience store several blocks away.

"What say we stop, get some film, and then go back to Dani's and take a whole roll?"

"Yeah!" Sawyer exclaimed, his face beaming with joy.

Though Dani had a million things to do now that the hired help had moved on, she chose to sit on her side porch and stare out at a ranch too big for one. Stepping indoors meant she had to endure the silence of the house. Stepping off the porch meant she had to get to work. Dani had enthusiasm for neither.

She hugged herself—a woman alone had no one else to do it—and fought tears of self-pity. He should've stayed, dammit! she told herself, intermittently angry and regretful. She'd all but begged him to and had received nothing for her efforts but macho pride and steely determination to move on and find a place of his own. Never mind that she had a ranch he was welcome to run.

He was going to be his own boss or die trying, and while somewhat of a maverick herself, and therefore able to appreciate his need for independence, she could not understand his obsession with owning land. It was as if his whole self-image hinged on being a property owner.

And doesn't yours? her conscience demanded.

"No," Dani replied somewhat crossly.

Then why are you so afraid he'll steal your ranch?

"But I'm not!" she exclaimed and knew it was true. Oh, maybe at first she'd been skittish. But now—now she believed she could trust him. And if she hadn't been such an idiot, if she'd told him the truth this morning about the size of her ranch, maybe he'd have been more willing to stay. Two hundred acres was hardly a challenge to a man like Ryan. But a thousand—now that was another matter.

But telling the truth now would not be easy—not when she'd been so long about it. He was bound to be hurt about the deception. And, she realized, even if he got over that, he might still turn down her offer of a foreman's job. He wanted more. He wanted a place of his own. He wanted to be her "equal," as he'd put it.

So sell him your place.

"Get real!" Dani scolded her conscience, even as the idea began to claim merit. She wouldn't have to sell all her land, just the portion now rented out. He and Sawyer could be her neighbors. She could pop over to their place every night with a casserole for their dinner. And every morning, after Sawyer got on the school bus, Ryan could pop over to her place for a quick roll in the hay.

"Yeah, right," Dani murmured, suddenly more depressed than ever. She wanted more than an affair with Ryan. And the point was moot, anyway. He and Sawyer were halfway to Wyoming by now... or at least a hundred or so miles down the road.

The loud crunch of frozen gravel on the driveway caught Dani by surprise. She glanced up, and seeing Ryan's truck brake to a halt not thirty feet from the porch, cried out with joy. Springing to her feet, Dani dashed down the steps to make the most of what had to be the best belated Christmas miracle ever—a second chance.

"What'd you forget?" she called out gaily, so glad to see them, so determined to keep them here.

"Pictures!" Sawyer exclaimed as he tumbled from the truck and into Dani's waiting arms. He hugged her with abandon, then stepped back, held up a camera and exclaimed, "Say cheese!"

"Cheese," she obliged, giving him a smile straight from the heart. Dani then raised her gaze to the truck, where Ryan still sat behind the steering wheel. He said nothing, but did give her a look that could've meant anything. Dani took a deep breath and turned her attention back to Sawyer. "Why don't you go to the barn and get a picture of *that* Dani, too."

"Okay." In a flash, Sawyer spun on his heel and headed to the outbuilding, leaving Dani and Ryan alone.

"Aren't you going to get out of the truck?" she asked, tucking her fingertips into the pockets of her jeans, stepping closer.

Ryan seemed to hesitate, then slid across the seat and got out through the passenger door, left open by Sawyer. He shut it and turned to face Dani. "Sorry about this, but I did promise..."

"It's okay. In fact...I'm really glad. I need to talk to you."

"And I need to talk to you."

"Oh?" Her heart began to hammer with hope—unreasonable hope, true, but hope all the same. "Well, age before beauty."

Ryan said nothing.

"That means you go first," Dani softly prompted, at which point he nodded as though his head—or was it his heart?—wasn't really in whatever he had to say.

"I stopped by to see Cliff on the way out. While we were talking, he, um, just happened to mention that you own a thousand acres up here. I was surprised to hear that, since

I've only seen two hundred of it. I think you deliberately misled me. I'd like to know why."

Dani winced. Clearly, this was not a man who pulled his punches. But that was okay. She was ready to confess, ready to trust, ready to sell.

"I did hide the truth, Ryan, but only because I didn't know you. I guess I thought you'd be like Mick. Now, of course, I know better and, believe it or not, that's what I wanted to talk to you about. Would you be interested in buying the eight hundred acres I've got rented out?"

"You mean, after going to all that trouble to protect your property, you're now wanting to sell it?" His tone said he thought she was crazy, and who could blame him?

"Only to you." She stepped close and laid a hand on his arm, which tensed to her touch. "And only because I—I—" Dani stumbled to a halt, took a deep breath and tried again. "Only because I love you."

Ryan stared at her for so long without speaking that she began to wonder if he'd even heard her stammered vow of love.

Or, hearing it, did he now wish he hadn't?

Dani swallowed back the lump in her throat, suddenly unsure about everything. "Ryan . . . ?"

"Actually, your offer to sell is not the first offer I've had. One of the men at the meeting last night tried to sell me some land, too, Dani. Only he had one thousand acres."

Dani caught her breath. "Someone around here?"

"A close neighbor, actually."

Her eyes narrowed in speculation. "Who? What land?"

"Duke Littlejohn is who, and I think you can guess what land."

Dani's mouth went dry. "You can't mean—"

"I do," he interjected with a brisk nod toward the east.

"Why that bastard!" Dani cried, furious with the stepfather who'd been nothing but trouble from the day he showed up on the ranch and began to seduce her mother. Floundering in a flood of bad memories, she doubled up her fists and wished she were a man and Duke Littlejohn were around so she could punch his lights out. "Well, if that doesn't take the cake. Trust that jackass to offer my land to a damn stranger instead of to *me,* the rightful owner."

Ryan flinched as if her clenched fist had actually connected with something—namely, his jaw. "Don't worry, Dani. This *damn stranger* might've been tempted, but he really knows the difference between right and wrong. I have no intention of buying Littlejohn's land *or any other land* in this godforsaken state. Now, if you'll excuse me, I've got a kid to round up. Wyoming waits and it's looking more like heaven all the time."

Oh no. Watching Ryan walk away, it Dani took all of two seconds to regret her outburst and put things in perspective. For some reason, he'd seriously considered buying the thousand acres adjacent to her ranch. She desperately wanted to believe that reason was love, even though he had not responded moments ago when she'd admitted how she felt about him.

Did he love her? Did he? And if so, mightn't the land provide him with the property that would make him an "equal" in his macho eyes and give him the freedom to admit his feelings for her?

Yes! her heart sang.

Whirling, Dani managed two steps toward the barn before Ryan strode from it, Sawyer in tow. She hurried to intercept them.

"Ryan, I'm sorry. I didn't mean—"

"Yes, you did." Ryan turned to Sawyer. "Get in the truck, son. It's time to go." Sawyer took one glance at his dad's flashing eyes and instantly obeyed. "We're leaving now," Ryan then said to Dani. "I suggest you call your stepfather and make an offer for that land. He's moving to Texas soon. He really wants to sell."

"Not to me, he doesn't, and I don't want it, anyway."

Ryan just laughed, a sound bereft of humor, then moved in the direction of the truck. Dani blocked his way with a quick step.

"No, really, Ryan," she said, catching his arm to keep him from running over her. "Even if he'd sell the place back to me, I wouldn't buy it. I don't need that much land. I can't even handle what I've got now, which is one of the reasons I offered to sell part of it to you."

"So hire yourself some help. Cowboys are a dime a dozen around these parts. With the fringe benefits you offer, you shouldn't have a bit of trouble finding one."

Dani caught her breath at the unexpected crudity. "I don't deserve that."

"No, you don't," Ryan replied with a heavy sigh. She could tell he wished he could take back those words and knew exactly how he felt. "And I apologize for saying that. I didn't mean it."

"Sure you did."

He shook his head. "No, ma'am, I did not."

"Are you saying that anger and frustration sometimes make people say things they don't really mean?"

"That's exactly what I'm saying," he replied and then tensed as though registering what he'd just admitted. Obviously disconcerted, he slipped past Dani and made steps to the truck, which he quickly climbed into. Heart sinking, she waited for the roar of the engine, waited for that big ol' truck to roll down her driveway and out of her life.

Instead, Ryan got back out of the truck and began to pat his pockets as though searching for something.

"Where are they?" he then demanded of Dani.

"What?"

"My keys. I left them in the ignition. Now they're gone."

"Well, don't look at me, cowboy," she retorted, even as she wondered if some gracious Christmas angel had managed yet another belated miracle—chance number three.

At that moment, Sawyer slid across the seat and got out of the truck to stand by his dad. "I've got the keys, and I'm never, ever going to give 'em back 'cause I don't wanna leave." The child—who'd never behaved this way before, if his father's shocked expression was anything to go by—punctuated each word with a so-there nod.

"You know I don't want to leave, either," Ryan blurted out. "But we have to, son. We just have to."

"And why is that?" Dani demanded, stepping close, grabbing a handful of his jacket in each hand. She tugged hard on it to make sure she had Ryan's undivided attention, and continued only when he looked her dead in the eye. "Duke Littlejohn's offered to sell you one thousand acres of land that isn't 'godforsaken' at all, but heaven on earth. Isn't that exactly what you've dreamed of all these years, exactly what you want?"

"I used to think so," Ryan admitted, capturing both her wrists with the fingers of one hand and pinning them to his chest. To Dani's surprise, he then slipped his free arm around her back and pulled her up tight. "Now...*now* I know I really want more."

For a moment, Dani couldn't speak. Was this it? The Christmas miracle to end all Christmas miracles? Her heart thudded in anticipation. She swallowed hard. "What more could you possibly want?"

"Your love and your life, that's what."

Dani's knees buckled with relief, and had Ryan not been holding her, she'd have landed in a heap—a happy heap—at his feet. "They're already yours, Ryan."

"Then I guess that does make us equals," he breathed, his husky voice music to her ears.

"Not so fast, cowboy," Dani still managed to reply. "We both have a thousand acres now, true. But unless I have *your* love and *your* life, we're nowhere near equal." She tipped her head back and gave him a tremulous smile. "Do I have them? Are they mine?"

"Forever," he promised and then kissed her. It was several glorious moments before he raised his head again and then just to whisper, "I love you, babe."

"And I love you," she replied.

"Like a friend, Dani?" Sawyer's question startled both Dani and Ryan, who'd long since forgotten they had a witness. "Do you love him like you love a friend?"

"More like a husband, actually," she replied, taking one last risk.

Sawyer, hopping from one foot to the other in his excitement, turned to Ryan. "And how do you love her, dad? Like a wife?"

"Exactly like a wife."

"Then you two can get married?" Eyes wide and pleading, the boy looked anxiously from one to the other.

"If she's willing," Ryan told him, softly adding, "Are you up to it, Dani? Will you have us?"

"Yes and yes again!" she exclaimed.

"Group hug!" Sawyer instantly yelled, throwing his arms up in jubilation, then burrowing between Dani and Ryan.

The air rang with laughter as they welcomed him, and on her soon-to-be stepson's face Dani saw all the joys of Christmases yet to come.

* * * * *

COMING NEXT MONTH

#1198 MAD FOR THE DAD—Terry Essig

Fabulous Fathers

He knew next to nothing about raising his infant nephew. So ingle "dad" Daniel Van Scott asked his lovely new neighbor Rachel Gatlin for a little advice—and found himself noticing her charms as both a mother...*and* as a woman.

#1199 HAVING GABRIEL'S BABY—Kristin Morgan

Bundles of Joy

One fleeting night of passion and Joelle was in the family way! And now the father of her baby, hardened rancher Gabriel Lafleur, insisted they marry immediately. But could they find true love before their bundle of joy arrived?

#1200 NEW YEAR'S WIFE—Linda Varner

Home for the Holidays

Years ago, the man Julie McCrae had loved declared her too young for him and walked out of her life. Now Tyler Jordan was back, and Julie was all woman. But did she dare hope that Tyler would renew the love they'd once shared, and make her his New Year's Wife?

#1201 FAMILY ADDITION—Rebecca Daniels

Single dad Colt Wyatt thought his little girl, Jenny, was all he needed in his life, until he met Cassandra Sullivan—the lovely woman who enchanted his daughter and warmed his heart. But after so long, would he truly learn to love again and make Cassandra an addition to his family?

#1202 ABOUT THAT KISS—Jayne Addison

Maid of honor Joy Mackey was convinced that Nick Tremain was out to ruin her sister's wedding. And she was determined to go to any lengths to see her sis happily wed—even if it meant keeping Nick busy by marrying him herself!

#1203 GROOM ON THE LOOSE—Christine Scott

To save him from scandal, Cassie Andrews agreed to pose as Greg Lawton's *pretend* significant other. The handsome doctor was surely too arrogant—and way too sexy—to be real husband material! Or was this groom just waiting to be tamed?

FAST CASH 4031 DRAW RULES
NO PURCHASE OR OBLIGATION NECESSARY

Fifty prizes of $50 each will be awarded in random drawings to be conducted no later than 3/28/97 from amongst all eligible responses to this prize offer received as of 2/14/97. To enter, follow directions, affix 1st-class postage and mail OR write Fast Cash 4031 on a 3" x 5" card along with your name and address and mail that card to: Harlequin's Fast Cash 4031 Draw, P.O. Box 1395, Buffalo, NY 14240-1395 OR P.O. Box 618, Fort Erie, Ontario L2A 5X3. (Limit: one entry per outer envelope; all entries must be sent via 1st-class mail.) Limit: one prize per household. Odds of winning are determined by the number of eligible responses received. Offer is open only to residents of the U.S. (except Puerto Rico) and Canada and is void wherever prohibited by law. All applicable laws and regulations apply. Any litigation within the province of Quebec respecting the conduct and awarding of a prize in this sweepstakes maybe submitted to the Régie des alcools, des courses et des jeux. In order for a Canadian resident to win a prize, that person will be required to correctly answer a time-limited arithmetical skill-testing question to be administered by mail. Names of winners available after 4/28/97 by sending a self-addressed, stamped envelope to: Fast Cash 4031 Draw Winners, P.O. Box 4200, Blair, NE 68009-4200.

OFFICIAL RULES
MILLION DOLLAR SWEEPSTAKES
NO PURCHASE NECESSARY TO ENTER

1. To enter, follow the directions published. Method of entry may vary. For eligibility, entries must be received no later than March 31, 1998. No liability is assumed for printing errors, lost, late, non-delivered or misdirected entries.
   To determine winners, the sweepstakes numbers assigned to submitted entries will be compared against a list of randomly pre-selected prize winning numbers. In the event all prizes are not claimed via the return of prize winning numbers, random drawings will be held from among all other entries received to award unclaimed prizes.
2. Prize winners will be determined no later than June 30, 1998. Selection of winning numbers and random drawings are under the supervision of D. L. Blair, Inc., an independent judging organization whose decisions are final. Limit: one prize to a family or organization. No substitution will be made for any prize, except as offered. Taxes and duties on all prizes are the sole responsibility of winners. Winners will be notified by mail. Odds of winning are determined by the number of eligible entries distributed and received.
3. Sweepstakes open to residents of the U.S. (except Puerto Rico), Canada and Europe who are 18 years of age or older, except employees and immediate family members of Torstar Corp., D. L. Blair, Inc., their affiliates, subsidiaries, and all other agencies, entities, and persons connected with the use, marketing or conduct of this sweepstakes. All applicable laws and regulations apply. Sweepstakes offer void wherever prohibited by law. Any litigation within the province of Quebec respecting the conduct and awarding of a prize in this sweepstakes must be submitted to the Régie des alcools, des courses et des jeux. In order to win a prize, residents of Canada will be required to correctly answer a time-limited arithmetical skill-testing question to be administered by mail.
4. Winners of major prizes (Grand through Fourth) will be obligated to sign and return an Affidavit of Eligibility and Release of Liability within 30 days of notification. In the event of non-compliance within this time period or if a prize is returned as undeliverable, D. L. Blair, Inc. may at its sole discretion award that prize to an alternate winner. By acceptance of their prize, winners consent to use of their names, photographs or other likeness for purposes of advertising, trade and promotion on behalf of Torstar Corp., its affiliates and subsidiaries, without further compensation unless prohibited by law. Torstar Corp. and D. L. Blair, Inc., their affiliates and subsidiaries are not responsible for errors in printing of sweepstakes and prizewinning numbers. In the event a duplication of a prizewinning number occurs, a random drawing will be held from among all entries received with that prizewinning number to award that prize.

SWP-S12ZD1

5. This sweepstakes is presented by Torstar Corp., its subsidiaries and affiliates in conjunction with book, merchandise and/or product offerings. The number of prizes to be awarded and their value are as follows: Grand Prize — $1,000,000 (payable at $33,333.33 a year for 30 years); First Prize — $50,000; Second Prize — $10,000; Third Prize — $5,000; 3 Fourth Prizes — $1,000 each; 10 Fifth Prizes — $250 each; 1,000 Sixth Prizes — $10 each. Values of all prizes are in U.S. currency. Prizes in each level will be presented in different creative executions, including various currencies, vehicles, merchandise and travel. Any presentation of a prize level in a currency other than U.S. currency represents an approximate equivalent to the U.S. currency prize for that level, at that time. Prize winners will have the opportunity of selecting any prize offered for that level; however, the actual non U.S. currency equivalent prize, if offered and selected, shall be awarded at the exchange rate existing at 3:00 P.M. New York time on March 31, 1998. A travel prize option, if offered and selected by winner, must be completed within 12 months of selection and is subject to: traveling companion(s) completing and returning a Release of Liability prior to travel; and hotel and flight accommodations availability. For a current list of all prize options offered within prize levels, send a self-addressed, stamped envelope (WA residents need not affix postage) to: MILLION DOLLAR SWEEPSTAKES Prize Options, P.O. Box 4456, Blair, NE 68009-4456, USA.

6. For a list of prize winners (available after July 31, 1998) send a separate, stamped, self-addressed envelope to: MILLION DOLLAR SWEEPSTAKES Winners, P.O. Box 4459, Blair, NE 68009-4459, USA.

EXTRA BONUS PRIZE DRAWING
NO PURCHASE OR OBLIGATION NECESSARY TO ENTER

7. The Extra Bonus Prize will be awarded in a random drawing to be conducted no later than 5/30/98 from among all entries received. To qualify, entries must be received by 3/31/98 and comply with published directions. Prize ($50,000) is valued in U.S. currency. Prize will be presented in different creative expressions, including various currencies, vehicles, merchandise and travel. Any presentation in a currency other than U.S. currency represents an approximate equivalent to the U.S. currency value at that time. Prize winner will have the opportunity of selecting any prize offered in any presentation of the Extra Bonus Prize Drawing; however, the actual non U.S. currency equivalent prize, if offered and selected by winner, shall be awarded at the exchange rate existing at 3:00 P.M. New York time on March 31, 1998. For a current list of prize options offered, send a self-addressed, stamped envelope (WA residents need not affix postage) to: Extra Bonus Prize Options, P.O. Box 4462, Blair, NE 68009-4462, USA. All eligibility requirements and restrictions of the MILLION DOLLAR SWEEPSTAKES apply. Odds of winning are dependent upon number of eligible entries received. No substitution for prize except as offered. For the name of winner (available after 7/31/98), send a self-addressed, stamped envelope to: Extra Bonus Prize Winner, P.O. Box 4463, Blair, NE 68009-4463, USA.